LILY IN THE STONE

J.P. STERLING

CHAPTER ONE

I think it was Mark Twain who said, "The two most important days of your life are the day you were born and the day you find out why." What about the day you find out you shouldn't have even been born? I think that day matters. Or finding out she's my mother. . . That matters.

*P*eter Arnold drove. One hour ago, he walked onto a car lot, wrote a personal check, and sped away in a black Ferrari F12 Berlinetta. It wasn't planned. He just needed a new identity––a new way to think. Playing the piano used to be how he sorted out his problems, but now, knowing what he knew, he just couldn't.

I can't play my piano. Her piano. My whole life I've done everything for her and she tried to kill me!

Peter pressed the gas pedal down generously, feeling a smooth acceleration as he watched the speedometer climb into three-digit speeds. He checked the rearview mirror as he switched lanes to pass a slow-moving semi-truck with two trailers. Pressing down on the accelerator even more, he cut in front of it. The knot in his stomach swelled.

Road signs flew by him so fast he became dizzy as he tried to read them. He dug the accelerator down even more, but then, the engine felt like it missed. He pulled forward and sped up only to rapidly slow down. He pushed the gas pedal lower, but the car kept slowing.

Peter looked down at his dashboard and saw his check fuel light was on. The gas gauge needle was buried in the negative and his car was slowing to a stop. He skillfully maneuvered the car to the side of the road, away from traffic, before it stalled completely. *Jerks. I spent all that money, and they didn't even give me a full tank of gas.*

Peter rubbed his forehead in frustration. He could call a tow truck, but he needed more than a tow. He needed to get his head right. He dialed Gwen, requesting a video chat.

"Hi, Pete." Her delicate face flashed on his phone. "What's up?"

"I need a ride."

Her button nose scrunched. "Where you at?"

"On the Interstate, somewhere west of Mara Gap. Maybe like twenty minutes out from you."

"By yourself?"

"It's sort of a long story."

Gwen's blue eyes clouded with worry as she studied Peter's face. "I can come get you, but it'll probably take me a little bit. Is that okay?"

"Yeah, I can't go anywhere. I'll be the guy in the black Ferrari on the side of the road."

"You got a new car?"

"I'll explain later."

Gwen ended the call, and her face disappeared.

Peter waited.

Forty-five minutes later, Peter sat in Gwen's more-than-gently-used, 1982 copper-brown Chevy Celebrity. The rust-colored interior fabric covering the ceiling of the car no longer stayed attached properly to the metal. It sagged in the middle, hanging down like a canopy, touching the tops of their heads. Gwen giggled when Peter tucked the extra fabric into the corner, only to have it fall back down, grazing the top of his head.

They listened to the only station that came in on the AM radio––an oldies station currently running an Elvis Presley countdown. "Who do you think is more likely to have staged his death–-Elvis or John Lennon?" Gwen asked.

"Are you into conspiracies now?"

"No, but I was watching this documentary on how Elvis faked his death to protect his family. It makes so much sense. There are sightings of him everywhere."

With a lopsided grin, Peter joked, "Yeah, and tomorrow I'm going to call you to pick me up when my UFO crashes."

"You're so funny." Gwen rolled her eyes and breathed into the mugginess of the air. With the air conditioner having long been broke and her window stuck and unable to open, Gwen sat sweating. A dampness set in on her hair that made her blonde curls stick to the tops of her ears. The creases by her nose glistened in the light of the setting sun. Pulling over to enter an exit, she said, "Here's a truck stop; let's get gas." She checked on him with a sideways glance and added, "I don't know if you're in a hurry to get back, but I can't breathe in here. Can we grab some food and wait for it to cool down?"

"Whatever," Peter muttered, and settled into another silence as he waited for her to pull into a parking spot. Then he got out, grabbed a red five-gallon gas can from beside the station, filled it, and placed it in Gwen's trunk. The trunk door floated back up when Peter shut it. Trying to slam it again, it took him a few times before it stuck. Laughing for the first time all day, he said, "This car's really a piece of junk, Gwen. If your cancer doesn't kill you first, this death trap will."

"Hey, chemo and stuff's expensive. This is all I can afford," she defended. "Not everyone can afford a Lamborghini."

"Ferrari. They didn't have any Lambos, but that would have been cool too." Then he gave her a sideways glance as they walked shoulder to shoulder toward the truck stop's café. "Hey, do you want it?"

Gwen squinted her eyes. "Yeah, sure. Funny."

"No, I'm serious. I probably won't need it long . . ." Sounding of hopelessness, his voice trailed off into nothing more than a whisper at the end.

Sharply halting her steps, Gwen carefully reached out, touching his arm softly. "What happened?"

Peter's eyes fled the other way. "It's all a joke. You'd never believe me."

She lifted her shoulders, hinting that she felt lost in this conversation, and said, "Try me."

"I don't even have the words."

Gwen rolled her lips inward, giving up for the moment. "Then let's go eat," she offered. After a moment of stillness, they trudged to the café, sitting on the same side of a booth as they always did since they were kids. Gwen ate french fries one at a time, slipping just the tip of the fry between her teeth, biting it off, and repeating. Peter loved the way she ate fries. He tried to eat them like she did but got impatient as he tossed the whole thing into his mouth at once.

Neither one felt like talking much. They watched videos on their separate phones as they sat until they were ready to get back into the car. When Gwen did finally drive back to Peter's car, she pulled up behind it and maintained a straight-forward stare, saying, "So, I get it. *Believe me*, I know what it's like. But I'm sort of not okay with leaving you alone right now."

Peter's gut constricted again, but he knew she understood him better than anyone. *That's exactly why I called you.* Turning toward her, trapping those brilliant blue eyes of hers, he beckoned, "Come with me. Follow me home, and we'll hang out."

"Okay," Gwen agreed softly, while continuing to hold her eyes in communion with his. It was a silent moment the friends had shared all too often in their many years of companionship, and when it was over, Peter jumped out of her car and hurried into his, leading her back to Mara Gap.

RESTING HIS HEAD ON HIS SEAT'S HEADREST, PETER LET HIS EYES DRIFT closed, and asked, "Have you ever met someone so, so selfish, self-absorbed, self-centered, and all about themselves?"

Gwen sat cross-legged in Peter's passenger seat, ready to listen. "You sure know a lot of adjectives to describe the same thing."

"No, I mean it. Like someone who only does things to help themselves. Expects some huge career, has no friends, and just hangs out by themselves all the time, wallowing in self-pity."

"Are you describing yourself?" Gwen's nose scrunched as it always did when she was confused.

"What?" Peter turned toward Gwen. "How could you ask that?"

"What do you mean? You said someone with no friends who just wants a career and self-pities. I get you're having a bad day, but this is your pattern. It sounds *exactly* like you."

"I have friends."

"Me, and Exa, who is twice your age." Gwen raised a challenging eyebrow.

"Well, yeah, I mean, I guess I never wanted any friends. I just liked piano . . . Man, you're right." He balled his hand into a fist and tapped it with force on his steering wheel. "I'm *just* like her."

"Are you talking about Exa? Are you still mad she left?"

"Oh, no. I'm over that. I saw her again."

"What did she do now?"

Peter glared out the driver's-side window. "It's not what she did. It's what she wouldn't do."

Gwen leaned forward, frustrated by his lack of details. "What won't she do?"

Peter's gut knotted in disgust as he readied to spit his words out, "She won't save my life." Then he hung his head low, feeling abandoned, knowing he had to accept the situation as his new reality, but it stung like white and blue fire.

CHAPTER TWO

*P*eter and Gwen padded quietly into his house, trying to go unnoticed. Half expecting his worried mom to meet him at the door, Peter was suspiciously confused when it was quiet. Then he wandered into the kitchen where Anne sat at the table with a cup of chamomile tea, browsing through a design website on her tablet. "Oh, I didn't even hear you come in. Do you want a snack?" She barely looked up.

Perplexed that she didn't show more concern, Peter's eyes slowly gravitated back to Gwen, who had the little twinkle in her eye and it suddenly all made sense. "You called her," Peter accused.

"Of course, I called her," she blurted out. "You're a pain in the butt for not calling her yourself. She's your mom."

"Did you tell her about the car?" Peter's gaze shot back to his mom who had a curl on her lips confirming she knew. "You're the pain in the butt," Peter said to Gwen, shaking his head at her secret shenanigans.

Anne raised her eyes, directing them toward Gwen. "Thanks, dear. I would've been worried had you *not* called."

Before she could comment to Peter, he cut in, "Mom, I can't, you know . . . talk about it."

"I know." Her eyes lowered respectfully. "I'm here if you want to talk, but I won't pry." Then her gaze slowly glided over Peter's body. She pursed her lip out, and asked, "Did you miss dialysis again?"

"Why?"

"You look puffy."

Crossing his arms self-consciously over his chest, he said, "Please don't do that."

"Sorry." Anne let her eye's fall back to her tablet, adding in a quieter voice, "I'll mind my own business."

"I didn't have dialysis tonight anyway," Peter went on. "Remember, I had it this morning because I skipped it last night."

"I believe you. Sorry, I'm just paranoid." Anne smoothed the conversation away, as she got up from her chair to rinse her cup out in the sink, placed it in the dishwasher, then tipped her head toward Gwen. "I hope you're staying the night. It's so late to drive back."

"It prolly is too late," she mulled while looking down at her jean shorts, "but I wasn't planning on an overnight trip."

"Oh, that's not a problem," Anne said, with a reassuring grin. "I'll grab you some of Marie's things to wear. She still has a drawer full of stuff in Macie's room for when she visits home." Without waiting for a rebuttal, Anne promptly left the kitchen to retrieve Gwen's stuff.

"Your mom's so sweet," Gwen expressed in a hushed voice. "You're really too hard on her."

Peter flashed his eyes to the ceiling then groaned. "I know she means well, but you know what it's like to have everything you do micromanaged, like she's afraid I'll drop over dead from getting a hangnail."

"Yeah, my mom's the same way." Gwen grinned her mischievous smile at Peter. "Hey, do you know what I want to do?"

Peter raised a curious eyebrow at her. "Go to sleep?"

"No," she continued in a hushed tone, "I want to go for a walk."

"Now?"

Raising her chin to peer out the kitchen window to do a fast weather check, she then confirmed, "Yeah, it finally cooled down and the stars are bright."

"Aren't you tired?" Peter threw out, hoping he could come up with an excuse for them to skip this outing.

"I'm always tired, but in a weird way, I'm wired too. I've been sitting too long." She leaned closer, letting her arm touch Peter's forearm, and urged, "Come on. I need to drive back right away in the morning, and we've hardly spent any time together. I'm not ready to say goodnight yet."

Peter's eyes cased down the adjacent hall. Then he matched her hushed tone, replying, "You know my mom won't like a cancer patient and a dialysis fugitive out of the house at this hour."

"Don't you turn eighteen soon?" Gwen quickly rebutted.

Peter's eyes dropped shyly to the floor. "Tomorrow."

Gwen quickly raised her hands to cover her cheeks. "I forgot! I'm so sorry." Then dropping her hand back to her sides, she insisted, "Well, then we have to go out. It's *your birthday* in like forty-five minutes. Let's celebrate it together."

"By going on a walk?"

Shrugging like she didn't have much to work with, she said, "What else are we going to do?"

"I don't know. Watch a movie." Peter's face remained indifferent, but Gwen pushed her lips out in a little pout until Peter relented, grumbled at her persistence, and said, "Fine."

Gwen leaned over, balancing on one leg as she studied the hall, still quiet with no sign of Anne. Then she whispered, "Let's just pretend to go to bed so your mom doesn't have to worry about it and then sneak out."

"Really?" Peter's tone was less than impressed.

"Come on, we never get to see each other."

"Yeah, I know." Peter crossed his arms, leaning back against the fridge, then after letting out a sigh like he was getting forced to go to the dentist, he muttered, "Fine, we can go."

"Okay, Gwen," Anne's voice cut through the air, and she reappeared into the room. "I found things for you." She produced a small stack of lounge clothes, handing them over to Gwen," then continued, "I was thinking you could crash with Macie in her room, but she's such a light sleeper; I think it's better to not disturb her tonight. Is it okay if we make up the couch?" Anne headed toward the couch in the family room, checking it for a blanket and pillow.

"Yeah, that's great," Gwen said, holding her eye's steady on Peter to make sure he wasn't going to give away their plan.

When Anne was finished fluffing the couch, she came back through the kitchen, and flashed a content but tired smile at her son and said, "Well, that should do it. You guys have a great night. I'm going to bed."

"Night," Peter and Gwen said in unison. The duo stood way too stiffly against the wall as they waited in silence until they saw Anne's bedroom door close, and the light darken. Then without waiting a moment more, Peter moved to the foyer, saying, "I'll get my cane."

"You still use that?" Gwen questioned even though she knew the answer because Peter had already pulled it out from the closet.

"It helps when I get tired." He defended, keeping his eyes low while he bent over to tie his shoes.

Gwen grinned daringly at him. "You need to toughen up.".

"What does that mean?" Peter asked amusingly but instead of waiting for an answer, he grabbed a gray hooded sweatshirt from the foyer closet, smelled it, and threw it on. "You need one?"

"Not if you have to smell it first." Gwen grimaced, but then went back to her previous comment, adding, "It just means you only hang out with people who know about your issues." She paused briefly, slipped on her flip-flops and opened the door, then picked up her thought again. "They treat you like you're broken. Maybe if you could forget about it every now and then, you might . . . live a little."

Peter followed on her heels down the walkway, commenting, "There you go with the no-friend thing again. What do you do that's so exciting? Homeschool?"

Ignoring his insult, Gwen folded her arms across her body. "It really cooled down, huh?"

"Here . . ." Peter removed his sweatshirt, hooking the hood on her nearest shoulder. "Just plug your nose." Gwen sputtered out a laugh but still eagerly slipped the shirt on.

"So, are you done with school?" Peter asked as they rounded the corner, landing them on the sidewalk, then offered, "I finished a couple months early to get ready for my tour . . ." His voice trailed off because the word "tour" caused a slow burn in his chest.

"I love your street. It's like one of those really great old streets you see in movies. I love how the trees line the road, creating a canopy," Gwen marveled.

"Eh, you didn't answer my question." Peter started to smirk, but stopped when he saw Gwen's serious face. "What's going on? Did you fail or something?"

Her eyes lowered to the sidewalk. "Sort of."

Peter's brows knitted together in question. "How do you fail homeschool?"

Keeping watch on the street ahead of her, she explained without showing emotion. "I did the accredited program online; it's tough. And I didn't fail. I just didn't finish. I quit."

"When did you quit?" Peter questioned, stunned because graduation was literally within weeks.

Gwen shoved her hands in the sweatshirt front pocket, picking up her walking pace. "I just quit. I don't remember when. It doesn't matter."

"Hey, wait up." Peter sped up to keep pace with her. "It does matter. What about college? I thought you were going to go to that culinary school. Will they accept you anymore without a diploma?"

"I'm not going to go," she tried to brush his comment away by quickly changing the subject. "Do you want to know what I really want to do?"

Not satisfied with her answer, Peter continued, "What do you mean you're not going to school? It's been your dream to have a restaurant since I met you." Then nudging an elbow gently into the side of her arm to make her smile, he added, "What about all those years you made me play restaurant with you and eat those burnt pancakes?"

"That was payback for having to listen to all your boring stories about your *celebrity* friend, Exa." Gwen darted a sideways glance at him, gritting her teeth. "Sorry, I didn't mean to bring her up."

"It's okay . . ." Peter didn't dwell on her comment because he was genuinely worried about Gwen, so he continued to press softly, "Why are you giving up on your dream?"

"What I really want to do is get a job at a chill coffee shop for the summer. I want to braid my hair every day before work, and meet cool people, and talk about books and music, and—"

Peter halted his steps—*seeing clearly the truth she was withholding, and it made his breath trap in his chest.* Since Gwen didn't stop with him, Peter just stared at her back as she continued to move forward, but somehow, he was able to force out his words, calling out to her: "Your cancer is back."

"Huh?" She flashed a quick glance back at him, then also stopped, waiting for him to catch up. "No. I just want to hang—"

"Gwen." Peter's feet fumbled forward, as he struggled for balance under the weight of his realization. When he resumed his spot by her side, he planted his feet close enough for an embrace and letting his eyes dig deeply into hers, he whispered, "Don't lie to me. It's back, isn't it?"

She swallowed and tried to act distracted by looking the other way, but Peter leaned over, trapping her eyes. Now he could easily see the hallow desolation inside them when she finally squeaked out, "It never really left."

His lips parted slightly agape, while his brows bent in worry. "Wait—" He started but then paused, considering. "You said they got it all." Then letting his head dip a slight measure toward her, he asked, "Did you lie to me?"

Sweeping her face to gaze the other direction, she innocently stated, "It wasn't an intentional lie. It's just, I was tired of people treating me like I was broken."

"People?" His head bounced back. "I'm not people. I'm your *best* friend. You should've told me."

In that moment, the emotion was just too strong, so instead of speaking, Gwen turned on her heel, abruptly resumed walking forward. Not surprised by her avoidance, Peter paced right by her side. After a of couple blocks of brisk walking, Peter broke the silence with a soft affirmation, "I'm sorry. I get it. I'm doing the same thing to you. It sucks to talk about it."

"Totally sucks." Her voice was even when she hooked her arm in camaraderie into his, slowing her steps again, but it wasn't slow enough because she could feel a tug from Peter falling behind her. He was looking at something--a house across the street with a For Sale sign. Without uttering a word, his eyes sparkled with curiosity, his feet changed directions and he pull her into the street.

"Come on. I'll show you something," he called, beelining to the back of the house where he went straight to a waist-level window next to the backdoor. He pressed the bottom of the window until a little pop sounded. "That's the latch," he explained. "It doesn't lock on this window." Then wrapping his fingers around the edge, he successfully pulled it open.

Gwen gasped, looking around to see if any neighbor's house had lights on. "Are you breaking into this house?"

Peter pulled himself up onto the ledge of the window, hanging his legs inside and turned back to see Gwen's caution stare. "No, I did this all the time. Exa was always forgetting her keys."

"This is her house?"

"Was," he sullenly explained. "She moved."

Then he reached his hand out to Gwen—who rolled her eyes—but reluctantly took his hand anyway while asking, "When are you going to let her go?"

Ignoring her plea, Peter pulled her safely inside but was overly quiet when he rested his cane against the wall, then crossed the room toward the stone fireplace on the opposite wall. Knowing the place like it was his own home, he ran his fingers along the mantel, looking for matches, but to his surprise he found none.

Starting to reach her limit of the Exa drama, Gwen propped a palm on her hip. "Really, I hate to be so blunt, but she's a snob. Why are we in her house?"

Shrugging his boney shoulders like he would never understand the female species, he explained, "I just wanted to show you." His arm floated out in front of him in gesture. "This is where my piano sat." Gwen squinted, trying to make out the shadows but even though the windows allowed light from a nearby streetlight to filter into the massive room, it was still too dark to see much. Gwen struggled to see before her, but Peter didn't need the light to know what it looked like—this room was his childhood. It was where his dreams were born.

Giving up on the darkness, Gwen pulled out her cell phone, turning on the flashlight. "Yep, it looks pretty creepy—like her."

Narrowing his eyes into mere slits, Peter asked, "Why are you so hard on her?"

Gwen snorted, like she was releasing a decade of disgust. "Why aren't you?" she shot back.

Inclining his head just enough so he could see past the bright light of her flashlight and into her face he asked, "What?"

"I don't get your obsession with her," she spouted back. "I'm sick of biting my tongue about her, but she used you to get a career boost."

"No, she didn't." Peter raised his voice, annoyed at her accusations. She gave me my career. Everything I have is because of her."

"Really?" Gwen pushed her bottom lip out and held her hand on her hip, then continued, "You followed her around like a little puppy even though she was always letting you down. I sometimes wish you'd never met her." Her voice dropped down into a mutter, but Peter could still hear perfectly when she added, "You might have had a normal life then."

"I wouldn't have met you."

Gwen's gaze softened. "I don't mean to be like this, but I always remember you being mad at her for *something*. Even now she is still upsetting you."

He hopelessly shrugged his shoulders. "What do you want me to do about it then?"

"Just let her go. Some people are just toxic to be around. She's one of them."

Peter leaned heavily on the fireplace hearth. "I don't have to," he sulked. "She let me go."

Like a soundless fairy, Gwen floated across the room, plopping down next to him, raising her eyes to plead, she said, "Will you *please* tell me what happened?"

Peter's eyes locked on his shoes, and he started to pick on his leather sole by his toe. After only a moment, he knew she was right, and he relented, ready to confide. "So, you know about how I was born. I told you all that after I got out of the hospital."

"Yeah, I remember."

"It's a long story, but I found the name of my birth mom and an address.

"Wait," Gwen immediately interjected, "I thought this was about Exa." Her eyes widened. "You found your birth mom and didn't tell me?"

"Just wait, it gets better," Peter sarcastically said. "So, this morning my mom drove me to the address we had found, and she was her."

Gwen's brows flattened. "Your birth mom?"

"No, I mean, yes. She was Exa. Exa was, or *is* my birth mom."

Gwen's eyes filled with despair. "I don't get it. How?" she whispered. "Does she know?"

"That's the crazy thing," he paused, shaking his head in disbelief, then lowered his voice even more while doing his best to explain, "I think she did know. When she saw me, she acted *strange*, not like herself at all." He rubbed the back of his head, hooking his hand on the back of his neck while he let his mind retrace his racing thoughts. Nothing made sense anymore and as he pondered the memories, he instinctively started to move, ending up back at the window. Now staring blankly out into the night, he picked up on his story. "I was stunned. *Clearly*, I was not expecting to see her. I instantly forgot why I was even there. Then I had like a flashing feeling in my brain, reminding me what her being there meant. I said the only word I could form—Elizabeth."

Letting out a sigh of misery like he had just learned his best friend died, he turned back, now bringing his eyes to face Gwen again. Still sitting on the hearth, she stared protectively back at him and filled in the silence by asking, "So, then what happened?"

"The color drained from her face. She told me I needed to leave and pushed me out the door. That's why I think she knew why I was there. But how?" Peter raised his hand in question. "And how could she deny me like that?"

"Maybe she didn't know." Gwen shrugged her petite shoulders, like she was equally confused. "Or maybe she was startled to see you or shocked you called her Elizabeth, or—"

"No," Peter cut her off. "I saw her eyes. She *knew* why I was there. The fact that I called her Elizabeth was enough to confirm that."

"It doesn't make any sense." Gwen threw her hands up in the air and crossed the room to join Peter at the window. "Why didn't she tell you if she knew?"

"My whole life doesn't make sense. Every time I get a grip on one thing that sucks, I learn something new."

"Wait a minute." Gwen raised her chin thoughtfully. "Does your mom know it was Exa?"

Peter's gaze glided back out the window and then down to the window ledge, spotting a box of matches pushed all the way up against the side of the wall on the window ledge. *Of course, that was where she always kept them, because she never had any furniture.* He grabbed them, holding them up. "I found matches."

Gwen raised an eyebrow. "You're going to burn the place down?" Then she took a step forward, like she was willing to assist. "I'm game. Let's burn these memories down."

"No psycho, I saw a log inside of the fireplace. I'm going to start a fire so we have some light.

"Um, we don't own this place."

"No, but maybe we should?" Peter flashed a surprised look toward Gwen. "Maybe I should buy it?"

Gwen paused like she was massively confused by Peter's sudden suggestion and when he didn't explain further, she asked, "Don't you think it's a little big for just you?"

Peter didn't hear her because he had already bent down in front of the fireplace, busying himself with trying to start a fire. Lucky for him, there was a small log in the corner and a small twiggy branch that was perfect to ignite.

"Who doesn't clean up after themselves before they move out?" Gwen asked, when she saw how the fireplace had been left.

"There you go again. You're so hard on her," Peter commented, more to himself because he knew Gwen wouldn't ever say anything nice about Exa. The he shook the match out and took the glowing twig and held it to the log. He blew slightly on the log, trying to stir the flame. Once Peter was happy with his blaze, he sat back down, facing Gwen. "Nice and warm, isn't it?"

Gwen relented in some of her stubbornness, sitting crossed-legged next to him. "It does look like she left the place in a hurry. Maybe she was running from something?"

"Yeah." He hung his head low and said, "Me."

"I doubt it, but you didn't answer my question. Does your mom know she's Exa?"

"No, I haven't told her anything. I just left Exa's house and told her I needed to walk home because I needed to be alone. She wasn't happy about it, but she gets something weird happened." Peter watched the flames dance around the log. A phone beeped. Gwen pulled hers out and read a text message. Her lips curled as she typed something back. "Is that my mom?" Peter asked.

"No, it's my mom." Gwen quickly stashed her phone back in the sweat-shirt pocket.

"Why would your mom text you at midnight?"

"She's just saying goodnight. Oh, midnight, Peter!" Her face lite up into an exuberance. "Happy birthday! Make a wish."

"Don't I need a cake for that?"

"Well, I don't have one. Humor me."

Peter stared blankly as he didn't know what to wish for. *Yesterday, I would have wished to meet my birth mother. Today, I wish I hadn't. I have money, a new car, family. I need a kidney, but that's not going to happen. Maybe the only thing I really need is friendship. Apparently, I suck at being a friend. I'm going to wish for better friendships.* Then he turned back to Gwen, and quietly said, "Okay, I wished, but it's a secret."

She winked. "Just as long as you tell me if it comes true."

Feeling exhausted from the emotional drama of the day, Peter was ready to think about something easier. He knew exactly what he wanted to get Gwen's opinion on. "So, let's talk about this house," he started. "I used to think it would make a great music school for kids like you and me. You know, sick kids. Or maybe just a school for lots of things, like if your dream is to go to culinary school, you could come here to learn to cook," Peter said.

"You mean like themed camps?"

"Yeah, exactly. It could be free for kids who can't afford it, and they could come here in the summer and learn something they love. Like a dream-come-true camp."

"Sounds amazing," Gwen said. "I can see it filled with all sorts of kids. It would give them a chance to meet someone like them, you know. It's always been easier being me, once I met you. Do you know what I mean?"

"Yeah, I know what you mean. I think I'm going to call a realtor in the morning to make an offer. This place is a dump. They'd probably give it to me to get it off their hands." Peter chuckled, but when Gwen didn't receive his joke, he turned his head back to her and asked, "What?"

"It's just, it's a good idea. I love it. But I hope you're not doing this to hold on to *her*. You can look at other locations."

"No, this isn't about her. This really is about me." His eyes searched out into the dark room, now glowing with firelight. "I used to daydream about having a place like this to go when I was little, but instead of it just being me and Exa, there would be other kids like me. Kids who actually *liked* me. I think it would have made a difference in my life. Maybe I would have had a chance for more real friendships. You know, like I have with you."

A cracking noise busted through the window, followed by the sound of rain. "That's thunder. It's pouring out." Peter got up and closed the window they had crawled through. He watched the streets fill with organic puddles of water. "Should I call a cab? We can't walk back in this."

"No, let's just hang out here. It's sort of cozy now." She took Peter's sweatshirt off, wadded it up like a pillow, and stretched out on the floor, closing her eyes, looking perfectly peaceful.

Peter smiled to himself. His body was tired, but his mind was racing. He had so many ideas about how to make this place into a school. He had already formed a charity last year to help fund music programs in schools, but this would take his cause to the next level. He had too much to plan out to sleep now. So, while Gwen rested, Peter planned until the first light of dawn crept in through the window.

Long after the fire had gone out, a chill filled the room finally waking Gwen. "What time is it?" She asked when she sat up, smoothing down her curls that stuck out in every direction. She grabbed her cell phone. "Ugh, I need to get going already; I have stuff going on today." Stretching as she got up off the floor, she added, "We should bust out of this place before someone sees us."

Peter sat up, rubbing his finger joints as he always did first thing in the morning, but he was quiet which made Gwen worry again. "Are you going to be okay if I leave?" She asked.

"Hmm-mm," Peter replied.

"Can you tell your mom? So that you have someone to talk to."

"I don't know."

"Please," she urged, touching his arm again in the way that always made him feel comforted. "I can't leave you if I think you're not going to be okay. If you don't tell her, I will."

After doing a quick examination of how he felt today, he realized he did feel slightly better about Exa, and he knew it had everything to do with Gwen. Trusting her—more than anyone—he stared fondly back at her and agreed, "I'll tell her."

"Promise."

"Promise." After a moment of letting Gwen give him her "you'd better or else glare," he got up casually, and grabbed his cane. "Can we call a cab? It's sort of far to walk."

"Don't be a baby, it's not that far." Gwen flashed a smile at him and added, "We can talk about your plans for the music school on the way." The she shot a quick glance out the window and asked, "Can we go through the door?"

"Sure," Peter agreed, feeling amused and they left together, making plans for the future like they'd both live forever.

PETER SLURPED UP CEREAL FROM A SPOON WHILE READING THE BACK OF THE cereal box like he always did during breakfast.

"Sammy called," Anne said, sitting across from him at the table. "He said your album sales were phenomenal, even without the tour."

"I think I'm gonna buy a house today. Can you come with?"

"Huh?" Her eyes widened. "What's wrong with living here? You just turned eighteen. You don't have to move out today."

"No, not to live in. For like an investment. I can tell you about it later." Peter explained in a rush as he stood, taking his bowl to the sink.

"If you want me to go with, I will," she offered. "I do need a ride in your new car."

Knowing his mom was doing her best to not pry, but also wanting to help, he quickly agreed. "Sure, I'll call a realtor and see when we can get together." Then he started to exit but Anne back after him.

"Hey, what do you want to do to celebrate your birthday?"

He lifted his chin and replied, "That."

"What?"

"Buy a house." *I think that's the perfect thing to do on your eighteenth birthday*, he thought and then found his way to the shower.

CHAPTER THREE

*P*eter texted Gwen the next day. *"I need to see you."*

Gwen: *"Okay. You come here?"*

Peter: *"No, I need to see you here. Do you want me to come pick you up?"*

"Gwen, are you still there." Peter texted when he didn't get a reply for thirty-minutes.

Gwen: *"Yes, still here. I have a dress fitting today. Do you need to talk?"*

Peter: *"No talking. I need to see you."*

Peter paced his bedroom floor unable to sit down. He jingled his keys in his hands, noting his key ring was getting heavier by the day—adding a new car, and two new properties in just three days.

"Alright, I can cancel plans. Be there in a couple hours, but I can't stay long," Gwen texted back.

THEN A COUPLE HOURS LATER, PETER BLEW THROUGH A STOP SIGN ON THE way to show Gwen his surprise.

"Where are we going?" Gwen asked.

"I met with a realtor yesterday about our school." Peter pulled over to park in front of his favorite coffee shop, The Steep and Brew.

"Our school?" Gwen glanced sideways at Peter. She finally removed

her hand from the doors she'd had a death grip on while he was driving and unlatched her seatbelt.

"You know, the one I was talking about?" Peter got out of the car and walked to her side to meet her.

Gwen stepped out onto the sidewalk, still a little nauseous from his driving and said, "It's a great idea, but I can't run a school. That's your dream."

"I know it's my dream." He pointed at the coffee shop and said, "but this is yours."

Gwen's nose wrinkled. "I need coffee?"

"No, you said this summer all you want to do is work at a coffee shop and meet cool people."

"I did say that . . . Oh, no." Her eyes quickly filled with dread. "I'm not applying for a job at The Steep and Brew. I can't work here."

"You don't have to *apply*. You can have it. I bought it for you." Peter's eyes shone brightly with anticipation as he waited for her to freak out in excitement, but that didn't happen. Instead, the color drained from her face, leaving her pale.

"What are you talking about?" Gwen fumbled for words.

"Don't you get it?" Peter probed. "Your dream is to *own* your own restaurant, not just work at a coffee shop. Why wait or give up on that when I can give it to you now?"

Gwen blinked and then blinked again, then finally blurted out frantically, "You can't buy me a coffee shop."

"I already did." He motioned back to the building before him. "I met with the realtor here to sign agreement papers on the school. While we were sitting here, the owner came up to my realtor and asked about putting the place on the market. I knew instantly it was divine intervention, and I made a cash offer."

Gwen hung her head low, rubbing her forehead. "You can't keep spending money like this," she said in a cautionary voice. "You have to think about your future."

"I'm thinking about my future. A decade ago you made a wish to meet me. I said, 'Yes' and that made your dream come true. Let me make this dream come true for you too."

"You can't buy me a coffee shop." Gwen shook her head vehemently. "It's too much."

"No, it's not," Peter insisted. "You can live in the school until we get that remodeled and ready to go. Why wait to make your dreams come true? Life's too short." He took a step closer to her, digging his eyes into hers. "We both know that."

Gwen swallowed hard. Her eyes that should have been elated as she celebrated her gift were instead filled with trepidation. "Peter, I can't move here. I have plans."

"Yeah, you said all you wanted to do was work at a coffee shop."

"I'm engaged," Gwen blurted out and then looked shyly at him with a sideways glance.

"Engaged in what?"

"Engaged to be married," Gwen repeated. "I'm getting married in August. I can't move here."

It was his turn to blink as her words seemed to flow out with an echo. Then he quickly looked down, fiddling with his car key ring. "You never said."

She shrugged her shoulders. "It didn't come up."

He snorted. "Yeah, like your cancer still being here never came up."

"That's not fair."

"Well, neither is you not telling me about your engagement." He turned slowly not knowing what he was even going to do but then he found himself walking back toward his car.

She followed him and reached out to touch his arm again. "Would it have mattered to you?"

Peter turned, releasing Gwen's grasp, and pointed to the car. "I know you're in a hurry to get back. I'll take you to your car."

"You were sick in the hospital," Gwen spit out. "I couldn't come flying in to brag about my good news when you were ill."

"No, it's cool. I get it." Peter rubbed his chin, wondering why this conversation was making him feel so weird. "I guess I thought, since I'm supposedly your best friend, you would tell me something like that."

"You are my best friend," she insisted, still trying to touch his arm, but he crossed out into the street, going around to his door, leaving her on the curb. "And I was always going to tell you. But you had a lot thrown at you lately."

"I get it." Peter opened his car door and slid inside. He turned the key, and the engine roared on.

Gwen slipped in next to him. "You know I can't play games with you," she said softly. "We have to be *okay*, or I'm not going home." She fixed her eyes on his, initiating that *look* that they always shared, and when she was convinced, things were better, she asked, "Are we cool?"

He gave her a slight nod. "Always." He held his fist up, waiting for their custom fist bump. She responded by tapping his fist with hers, and then quietly pretended to make it explode. Peter watched her relax into her seat, but he couldn't let the tension he felt go. There was a knot in his stomach, aching like he had been punched. He didn't recognize the feeling, but he knew it meant he had to get away from her. He shifted the car into gear and sped out, pushing Gwen all the way back in her seat as she squealed and gripped the door.

CHAPTER FOUR

a photo album rested in Peter's lap as he flipped through pages of his childhood. Anne lightly tapped on the open bedroom door. Peter flicked the book closed and set it down. "Come in."

She sat on his bed next to him and said, "I've barely seen you these last few days. How are the real estate deals coming?"

"Fine." He kept his chin tucked while he explained, "I'll have to find a manager for the coffee shop though. Gwen can't move here cause she's getting married."

Anne smiled thoughtfully. "I didn't know she was going with anyone."

"Me either." Peter felt the knot in his stomach that had been there most of the day. He realized now that it got tighter when he thought about Gwen with *some guy*.

Anne's brows flattened when she asked in an even tone, "How does that make you feel?"

"It's fine," he said flatly.

Anne hesitated for a moment and then asked, "Are you fine or are you confused?"

He scowled and shook his head in annoyance. "Why do you always do that?"

"Do what?"

"Ask me a question to answer a question. It's like you are twisting my words."

"I didn't know I did it a lot. Sorry."

He breathed heavily, like he had been trapped under water for a little longer than he was comfortable holding his breath. "I guess I'm a little confused. Like, she never said anything. I didn't even know she was dating anyone."

"Well," Anne's brows lifted in an encouraging manner when she said, "Gwen probably didn't want to drag you into her boy drama." Then she picked up the photo album and began flipping through it. Not being able to resist a smile, she fondly pointed to the first photo and recalled, "This is when we went out to eat at that Japanese sushi place in New York." She chuckled. "Do you remember that waiter?"

"Yeah." Peter reminiscently laughed. "He really didn't know what was going on, did he? He kept bringing us courses of food we didn't order. None of it was even on our bill."

"I tried to tell him to take it back, but he just got mad and went back to the kitchen and brought us more food. It was ridiculous that he got mad at us."

Peter chuckled again this time with a little more life behind it. "There must have been a glitch in their computers."

Anne rested a hand on her belly. "I was so full."

"I was sick."

"You did get sick, didn't you?" She looked over at Peter, but when she saw his face, she knew they weren't really talking about sushi. She placed a hand on his knee and said, "It's okay to be confused about Gwen's engagement. She's a big part of your life."

His brows knitted together, and his voice floated out. "It just feels different. I always thought of her as *my* Gwen. I know that sounds weird, but thinking of her with some guy . . . I don't know if it will be the same."

"She will still be your friend even after she's married. If that's what you want."

Peter looked down at his hands. "I don't know what I want."

"Well, you don't have to decide everything today. Sometimes these things need time to sort them out."

"I'm not sure there will be any time," he said with a tone of worry. "It seems like it's all happening fast."

"It'll work out. Trust me," Anne said, patting his knee one more time. Then like she knew he was hurting, she changed the subject, "Maybe Tane and Paul would like to run the coffee shop together? It seems like something they could do around their college schedules."

Peter perked up a little, sitting straighter. "Really? I thought Tane was coaching with the high school?"

"He is, but it's not enough hours to pay for anything. He told me the other day he wanted something else. Paul has another year of school left because he decided to get his CPA, so he might be up for it too."

"Yeah, that might work. I can ask." Peter rubbed his thumb joint out of habit. "I guess I should've asked her before I bought it for her."

"You didn't know," Anne said in a quiet voice barely above a whisper. Then raising her tone to hold some optimism, she added, "You had a good idea. It's still a great idea. Very sweet of you. And it may turn into a great investment."

Peter looked at his mom. She had her hair wrapped up in a messy bun on top of her head, and little makeup. She looked tired under her eyes, but happy. Most of all she looked like she cared and that meant a lot to him. Figuring it was time, he said, "Hey, Mom?"

"Yeah."

"If I tell you something, do you promise to not freak out?"

"I'll try."

"She was Exa." Peter watched his mom's expression, but he didn't see the shock lights flutter in her eyes. He felt something like his heart dropping an inch in his chest from disappointment. Then his jaw lowered slightly when he diagnosed her face. "You knew it was her?"

Anne's shoulders noticeably stiffened.

"You knew it was her," Peter repeated softly, confirming the truth. "How could you keep that from me?" His voice squeaked. "Did you know the whole time?"

"I didn't know the whole time," she quickly defended. "I just found out."

"How long?"

"Only moments before you."

Peter narrowed his eyes, glaring at her.

"I swear," she added. "Your dad called me when I was literally in the van outside her house. It was too late for me to catch you."

Peter's brows raise to the ceiling. "Dad knew?"

"No, he just found out too. He hired a detective while you were in the hospital. I had no idea about *that* either. He was hoping to find your birth mom before we told you about everything. We wanted there to be a silver lining."

"How did he find her?"

"Don't tell anyone." Anne leaned forward, trying to shield her voice from any of the other kids who were home and may overhear, "but he dug through the clinic records. Years ago, the old paper records from the abortion clinic were moved to the basement of the hospital. No one is down there monitoring that area. It's illegal to just look up patients for your own purpose, but he really didn't care. He said he would rather go to jail than you know . . . the alternative."

"It was that easy?"

"Well, no. It took a while, but he found a record for a lady who had a procedure on your birthday. He gave the name to a private detective, and they only found her that morning. I was sort of mad myself when I found out he was hiding all this from us, but I understand he didn't want to get our hopes up."

"It would have been nice of him to tell me before I went over there."

Anne's eyes paced Peter's face, then she asked in a much quieter voice, "What did she say when you told her?"

"I didn't have to tell her." He let his eyes drift closed. "She knew. She pushed me out the door."

"How do you know she knew?"

Opening his eyes back to a mostly normal expression, Peter flatly explained, "She's terrible at faking any emotion, and it was all over her face."

Anne sighed, like the seed of fear she'd been suppressing was starting to swell. "Well, give her some time. She was bombarded with all this. You have no idea what she knows. Maybe wait a week and I can call her."

Peter's face grew an unnatural crimson color.

"Or not," Anne said, taking his hand. "Honey, I don't know what it's like to be you. *And I'm lost.*" Her eyes carried the burden of her thoughts. "I know you don't want me to freak out. I'm going to try not to." Then in a voice that was so quiet Peter had to read her lips to fully comprehend it, Anne added, "I'm just going to let you lead us on this one."

Peter squeezed his mom's palm, wishing for a moment to be transported back to the day when everything had been made better by holding hands with his mom. He matched her tone, but looked at her lovingly when he replied, "Thanks, Mom."

CHAPTER FIVE

One mundane week later, Peter got a surprising text.

Gwen: *"Pete, I changed my mind. I would love to work at your coffee shop."*

Peter: *"I found someone else."*

Gwen: *"Who?"*

Peter: *"Paul. He's a business major."*

Gwen: *"Can I help? I really want to."*

Peter: *"Why?"*

Gwen: *"Because, like you said it's my dream and why wait. And because I know food. Paul can't cook to save his life."*

Peter: *"Good point. Yeah, there is enough work for you if you want to help."*

Gwen: *"I do."*

Peter: *"Okay."*

Gwen: *"Can I still crash at your creepy hospital house?"*

Peter: *"Sure. I close on the shop next Friday. Work starts the following Monday."*

That was the extent of the conversation that changed Peter's plan for the summer. Well, more Gwen's life than his as Peter just showed up daily for his decaf Americano and to stare at the fish tank.

A week into their new business venture, Peter read a book in what had become his usual spot—the cracked leather chair near the front door that had an adjacent art deco-coffee table that made the perfect foot stool—when the hinges on the wood door whined from the door opening. Out of the corner of his eye, he saw a tall man with an athletic build, walk through the door, looking around the room as if he were lost.

"Can I help you?" Peter asked from behind the book he was reading.

The mans' eyes were fixed on the front counter when he answered, "I'm looking for someone."

"Brad!" Gwen's voice rang through the air, and a moment later she manifested right in front of the man and flung her arms around him.

Disgusting. I know who Brad is now. Peter scowled as he dug his eyes back into the pages of his book, but he couldn't ignore that

Gwen had now turned to Peter with a beaming smile and said in a soft voice, "I want you to meet my fiancé."

"—Brad," Peter cut her off, still not raising his eyes to meet either of theirs. "I heard his name when you squealed it out for the whole building."

Even with his eyes planted firmly on the book in front of him, it was easy for Peter to notice that Brad had big perfect white teeth behind his giant smile. *A big, dumb, Brad smile,* Peter thought.

"It's great to finally meet you," Brad said, with an air of confidence. "Gwen talks about you all the time. I would be jealous if it didn't sound so much like she was talking about her little brother."

Peter allowed his eyes to drift up to barely graze Brad's face. "Hm, I didn't even know your name until now." Then, feeling like things were about to get awkward, he excused himself by saying, "Sorry, but I need to take off. I have to get over to the school to make sure my contractors showed up. They aren't the most reliable group of guys." Then he stood up, careful not to wobble, not wanting to show weakness in front of Brad. He wasn't exactly sure why he cared, but Brad's presence had made him uneasy.

"Wait, Peter . . ." Gwen sidestepped to block him from leaving. "That's what Brad's here for."

"Huh?"

Gwen continued, "I know you've been having issues with the construction crew being understaffed. Brad and I have been missing each other so much, and well, you see, he has a background in carpentry. He used to work at his dad's cabinet shop. I was hoping you could give him a job helping the crew, so he could stay in town. That way we could see each other more. And you'd have someone reliable watching things over at the school." Gwen batted her eyelashes at Peter the way she did when she wanted to get something from him.

You want me to hire this big, dumb, Brad? I don't like the way he looks at you, Peter argued internally while standing tall, with a forced grin on his face as he tried to find a way out of this dilemma.

"He's a great worker, Gwen continued, "and if you don't like him, just say the word and he'll be gone."

Peter stayed silent.

"Please, do it for me?" Gwen pleaded with her eyes, just as hard as her words.

Peter couldn't say no to her—it was an impossibility. She had these wild blue eyes—cerulean like that of an old soul—yet angelic enough to think she could never do anything wrong. Defeated, he mumbled, "Fine." Then without even letting a stray eye encourage Brad in anyway, he edged toward the door, grumbling "I'm on my way over there now. I *guess* you might as well come with me and I'll show you the job."

"Thank you so much." Brad eagerly followed him outside. Even when the door closed noisily behind them, Brad continued, "Really, thanks, man. I won't let you down."

"We'll see," Peter murmured under his breath, but loud enough because he wanted Brad to hear it. Then he shot a sideways glance and asked, "Do you have a car?"

"Yeah, that's mine." Brad pointed to a late-nineties rusted-out truck that was complete with a set of homemade exhaust stacks protruding from the box.

Peter chuckled internally. *Of course, that's his big, dumb truck.* "Follow me." Peter muttered as he veered off the curb and climbed into his Ferrari. He purposely hurried through the motions of getting belted and starting the car, then sped away, forcing Brad to struggle to keep up.

. . .

THE NEXT DAY AT THE COFFEE SHOP, PETER SLOUCHED INTO A RECLINING position in his usual chair by the door, reading his same book, when it was Gwen's turn to walk in with a big, dumb smile on her face. *Nice. That stupid Brad smile is contagious.* He pulled his book up closer to his face, burying his nose, and vowed not to look at her.

"Morning, Pete," Gwen sang out as she proceeded to look even dumber by twirling in a circle—her long, floral maxiskirt fanned at the bottom. Then after an abrupt stop directly in front of him, she pushed her hand in front of his face and wiggled her fingers.

"What?" Peter scoffed from behind his book.

Gwen continued to wiggle her fingers. Peter narrowed his eyes, suspicious of her behavior and he examined her fingers move, and then he saw *it* – a gold band. A microscopic tiny thread of a gold band with a spec of something so small on it, it made him snort. "Is that your engagement ring?"

"Don't you love it? Brad got it for me with the advance you gave him yesterday. *Thank you so much.* I just looove it. I'm never taking it off." She twirled around again and continued to dance as she made her way back to the counter.

"I gave him that advance so he could get some good work tools," Peter called back flatly.

"Oh, he did. He got everything he needed. We got some really good deals. Don't worry."

He forgot the diamond on your piece of thread. Ha. I could've got you a diamond the size of a doorknob.

"Hey, Pete?" Gwen asked, from behind the counter as she tied on her apron.

"What?" Peter responded with caution as he was already thoroughly disgusted in the way this morning's conversation had been going.

"I was thinking of doing like an open mic night thingy here. All the cool coffee shops in the big cities do them. It could be like part of our grand opening."

"Okay."

"Would *you* start it off?"

Peter alerted, raising his eyes from his book, arching one brow above the other as he stared back at her. "Huh?"

"Would you play piano? It would be very chill and casual."

A lump appeared in his throat. "I don't know. I'm sort of taking a break from playing." He pulled his book even closer to his face. At this point, the book was so close to his face, when he tried to read it, he went cross-eyed; but he needed it— his book was his shield from this stupid conversation.

"You can't take a break from piano. That's like me taking a break from breathing." The till rang as Gwen opened it to count the money.

She pulled out a stack of ones and started counting them one by one and when she didn't say anything more, Peter responded by asking, "Is it?"

"Oh, *good grief.* Why do you have to wallow in everything all the time? It's just for fun. Just play some fun coffee shop music. Unless you think you're too good for it?" She glared at him, but not in a disapproving way. Her eyes gleamed like each little sparkle was its own individual dare.

"Fine." Peter sighed, like he had been trapped in a minefield and the only way out was to hitch a ride on the rope that had been dropped down from the enemy copter. Then he let his book flop down onto his lap with the same desperation. "When are you thinking about doing this terrible idea?"

"It's all set up for next Friday." Her eyes steadied on her till as she replaced the dollars and grabbed coins to count.

"Oh, I see you already planned it."

"Yep, and Sammy already has a production crew set up to film it." Gwen's lips curled into that brilliant grin, that Peter was recently learning was also the grin that made him do things he didn't want to do.

"You're a poophead," Peter said, using the childhood nickname he used to call her.

"I know."

THE FOLLOWING MONDAY, PETER TOOK ANNE TO CHECK ON RENOVATIONS at the school. When they saw the vast floor plan, Johnny and Macie,

Peter's siblings, burst out running as if they were dancing in a never-ending candy land.

"Hey, you two!" Anne hollered after them. "Don't be running around. It's not safe. There's nails and boards and stuff everywhere."

"What?" Johnny's voice could be heard calling from the opposite side of the room, already ducking in a corner and counting for hide-and-seek.

"I said, don't run. And watch where you are going."

"Okay, Mom." Johnny stuck his head back into the corner and resumed counting.

Peter chuckled, like his mom was being ridiculous. "I don't think he will get hurt back there."

"You never know." Anne sighed, then tipped her head to a cot pushed up against the wall, covered in a hot-pink Elvis Presley fleece blanket. "Hey, whose stuff is all this?"

Peter took one look at the blanket and rolled his eyes. "I thought she was over that phase."

"Who?"

"That's Gwen's. She's been obsessed with him as far back as I can remember."

Anne winked at him. "She's always had great taste in musicians."

"She's staying here," Peter explained. "I guess she must have moved her stuff down here since there's so much construction upstairs. Come on." Peter crossed the room, heading upstairs, "Let me show you the suites they're creating up there."

On the second-floor landing, Brad hung with one foot on a ladder, trying to tie in a huge hanging globe light fixture.

Peter grabbed the bottom rung of the ladder to steady it and called up to him, "Woo, Brad, is that safe?"

"I'm cool. I do this all the time," Brad eased over his concern. Peter tried not to notice that his arms were extremely conditioned and tan, but that was hard to do since they were fully on display with Brad wearing a sleeveless muscle shirt that said, "The Gun Show Starts Now."

He pivoted on his heel, passed through the nearest door and called back to Anne, "Come on in here."

Anne was right on his heels, her jaw dropped when she saw the bedroom, remodeled to resembled something out of a bed and breakfast magazine. The walls were retextured with a soft finish, and a light-gray coat of paint. The wood flooring had a fresh stain, and new light fixtures glowed, creating a cozy, warm atmosphere. "I love it," Anne exclaimed as she turned around. "It looks so comforting in here."

Brad's voice boomed from the door. "I'm not as good with colors as I am with fixin', so Gwen's been helping me with the color pallet. Here's the fabric swatches she picked out with me last night." Brad handed Anne a bundle of fabric. "We want to use this one for the window covering, and this one for that couch." He pulled out a swatch with soft yellow pansies. "Gwen thought it would be cool to have a fun, funky fabric to tie all the colors together."

Peter smashed his lips together, hard. He wanted to dislike Brad, but this moment was painful because he had to give him at least a little, tiny bit of credit. He had accomplished more in his first week than his entire crew got done in three weeks. The more dreadful part was that not only was he fast, but Brad had also completed everything beautifully—which could only mean, Peter could not think of a single reason to fire him. "It looks good," Peter said, reluctant to give him a compliment.

Anne set the fabric swatch down on the chair. "I like how it's turning out. This is a wonderful project."

"I'm happy with my decision too," Peter said, making sure to not accidentally compliment Brad again.

"Hey, I forgot," Brad motioned for them to follow him out into the hall. "Come look at what we found in the closet." Brad led them out of the room where there was a television-sized box. "There were like twenty black dresses, all still hanging up. All the shoes to match were there, too. It looks like a witch used to live here."

Anne smirked, and her eyes fled to Peter, who spoke up who had nothing more to say but offered, "Possibly."

Brad closed the flap on the box. "Yeah, maybe you can donate them to the thrift store. They'll be popular for Halloween." Then he straightened up again and motioned to the room across the hall. "So, all the rooms up here were empty, except this one. It was completely furnished. It's so strange, like somebody fled."

Strange doesn't even begin to explain her. Peter didn't want to talk about Exa and thankfully the conversation shifted from the sound of Anne digging in her purse for her keys. When she found them, she jingled them once in her hand, and gave a final look at her son. "I'm glad I got to see the progress."

"I'm glad you could see it, too. Thanks for coming," Peter said.

"I need to go find your siblings and get going. They have swimming lessons."

"Yeah, that's fine. I gotta get back to work too."

Anne descended the top step, on her way down, but called back over her shoulder, "Okay, I'll see you for dinner then?"

"Yeah," Peter called back to her but walked in the opposite direction to go down the back staircase, hoping to run into his foreman but he never found him. Instead, he found that the railing had been removed to prepare for a new one. These stairs were much steeper than the front ones, and not a big deal to a person with normal balance but they looked like a bad idea to him. Not wanting to have to go back upstairs and risk running into Brad and then have to explain to him why he couldn't go down the back stairs, he stubbornly clung to the wall as he lowered his legs one at a time, trying not to stumble. He watched his feet as he placed them carefully on each step and then finally the bottom landing. With a breath of relief, he removed his hand from the wall, and when his eyes raised, he was suddenly shocked to find a figure standing in front of him. Exa had let herself in and was watching him.

CHAPTER SIX

"Hi," Exa said softly, flicking her wrist to flash her hand in a wave. She also not-so-conveniently blocked the stairwell; Peter was stuck. "I heard this place sold," Exa offered. "My friend mentioned who bought it, and I had to see for myself."

Peter folded his arms and leaned back against the wall. "Did you come for your clothes?"

"No." Exa nervously adjusted her purse strap to rest higher up on her shoulder. "I didn't think about that."

"My guys cleaned out a box of your stuff. I can have them load it in your car, if you want."

Exa waved her hand at the construction mess behind her. "Pe ta, what are you doing?"

Peter shuffled his legs, wishing he could get around Exa without having to smash into her, but she did her best to center herself in the narrow halls, leaving no room for anyone to pass. "I'm remodeling it into a school."

"You hate school," she immediately shot back at him.

"Yeah, well a different kind of school. One for kids to come to learn about music," he rambled out in one breath, and then feeling the frustration bud in his chest, he let it slide right out of his mouth by blurting out, "Why are you here talking to me about this?"

Her perfectly groomed brows caved down. "What do you mean?"

"I mean, it's a little awkward considering the last time I talked to you," his words were sarcastic, but his tone held desolation.

Inching toward him, a single step, she spoke in a concealed tone, ". . . About that."

"Don't." He leaned to the left, trying to push passed her, but she didn't budge. "Do you mind?" His eyes narrowed into slits but he was at least able to look at her this time when he said, "Please, I'm busy right now."

"We need to talk about this."

"There is nothing to say."

"Give me a chance to explain."

"Then what?"

"Then, you decide what you want to do next."

Peter let out a disgruntled sigh, knowing that Exa was stubborn. "Alright," he finally agreed.

"Can we go someplace private?" Exa asked just as a saw turned on in the background and she had to raise her voice.

Peter motioned out the backdoor, and said, "Outside." Finally, Exa moved to the side, so they could both exit.

"Is that your car in the driveway out front?"

"Yep." Peter pushed his hands in his sweatshirt front pocket. "You know, I really don't have the stomach for small talk. I'm not trying to be a dick, but what happened? I mean everything--all the years. I want to know."

Exa dropped her purse and sat next to it on the cement steps that overlooked the private backyard. The steps were separating from the house and a huge space created a crack between them. "Be careful," Exa warned as she watched Peter step over the crack. He pulled his hands out of his pocket to hold onto the door frame. His joints were more knotted than normal since he stopped playing piano weeks ago. He could feel her looking at his hands. He shoved them back into his sweatshirt pocket and sat next to her.

"How are you?" She asked.

"You don't get to ask me that."

"That's fair." She looked away. In a weak voice that she was obviously forcing out, she asked, "Where do you want me to start?"

Still completely upset about everything, there was one thing that bothered him most so in a tone of accusation he started, "Did you know?"

After a long pause she said, "I don't know when I *knew* knew, but I know a part of me felt a pull. I could never explain it; I never thought I'd have to."

"You said you would." His voice was now flat and even when he insisted, "I want to know."

"I was a different person back then. I was young. I had just met Ambrose."

"Is he . . .?"

She nodded, keeping a straight-forward stare. "We weren't serious then, but I knew I loved him. He had this presence that was captivating, and not just on the stage. I was completely enamored. We were both struggling to get into the business. He had made some contacts and was building his career faster than I. I wanted a family," her voice trailed off to a whisper and she added, "he didn't."

"So, that was that? You didn't want a family, so you went to the clinic?"

"No, it wasn't like that," she said firmly. "I wanted to keep you. I prayed to God for a miracle for him to change Ambrose's mind, but my prayers went unanswered. So, I decided to have you on my own. About that time, he got the break he was waiting for and he left for New York. I moved back here from Chicago. I had an apartment lined up. It was a rat-invested dump, but it put a shingle over my head. I started to work with kids, doing music therapy to earn a little income. It was working out—"

Peter cut her off, and said, "—Then you changed your mind?"

"No, I never changed my mind; I just . . . I couldn't do it."

"What do you mean?"

"Ambrose refused to let me have you even though I swore I wouldn't want anything from him. When that didn't work, he changed his tune all together. He said if I didn't have the baby, he would marry me, and we could start a family after we had our careers established." Exa dropped her head into the palm of her hand. "It sounds so stupid now. I was so young and so worried about my career—"

"—Then you changed your mind?" Peter cut in again.

"I never changed my mind! *Stop saying that.* I wanted you, but it was an impossible choice. Ambrose was threatening me if I didn't do it, and he was offering me a way out, but I didn't do it. I stayed here and worked." She turned to him, the bottom of her eye lids were moist now as she remembered out loud, "I bought a crib and some baby clothes."

Peter could see Exa's eyes were layered in affliction, but he refused to engage her.

"I felt you move. You moved a ton whenever I played the piano. I just knew you were going to be a musical genius."

"I think you're stalling. We both know it didn't end on this note."

She waved her hand, like she was trying to move away from the hard part of the story and said, "Short story is I was broke. I learned what the medical bills were going to cost, and I didn't have insurance. Ambrose never stopped pressuring me. I told him about the medical bills. I was so *stupid* to say anything. He said he would give me money if I agreed to meet him." Exa shook her head. "Stupid me, I told him where to come. He showed up at my house and beat me up."

Peter turned his head to meet her gaze. "What?"

"He tried to kill me. He said he refused to have a kid ruin his career, and if I didn't have the procedure, he would kill me. He drove me to the clinic. Gave the doctor a load of cash as I was well past the time frame for a normal procedure, and he left me there." She rolled her bottom lip in and after a short hesitation, she added, "He didn't even give me a ride home."

"So . . . you married him after that?"

"I'm ashamed to admit it now, but he had such a hold on me. I was naïve. Now I know better. He's a monster."

After a long moment of dense silence, Peter spoke, "I don't think I ever thought you were happy in your marriage, but I didn't know he was like that."

"Nobody did. Two celebrities in marital bliss is what everyone saw. He threatened to kill me if I ever left him. He's crazy. I knew he would." She motioned to her former house behind them both and said, "I came here to hide."

Peter's lips parted in awe, as he strung together some of his most confusing memories. "That explains so much. I always thought it was weird that you chose to squat here when you could buy a mansion."

"Things are usually not as they seem."

"So, when did you know who I was?"

"It sounds crazy, but it was always there. Something just felt 'off' about you, but I know now, I was right about so much."

"What do you mean?" Peter's confusion deepened and he dug his eyes into hers as he was no longer afraid of the truth because he desperately needed to hear it.

She let her eyes linger on his while she resisted the memories that were so painful to her. Knowing he needed this information and believing it was fair to tell him, she mustered up the strength to continue, and with a tear-filled voice, she recalled, "Pe ta, after the procedure, the doctor wrapped you in a blanket. I swore I saw you move. The doctor mumbled some stuff and then handed you to the nurse who ran out of the room." Exa closed her eyes. "One part of my heart knew that you were alive, but I didn't listen to it because all I heard was the other part of my heart dying."

"If you knew I was alive, why didn't you say something?" Peter nervously rubbed his finger joints, feeling anxiety rush through his veins.

"I didn't let myself believe it. The doctor insisted everything was normal. The years that followed were a blur. I moved in with Ambrose. Got married. His connections led to my career. I toured, recorded, and made more money than I knew what to do with. I didn't think about what had happened. It hurt too much." She picked a tall dandelion that was growing next to the step and twirled the stem with her fingers. "On the outside, I looked happy. In the inside, I was living a nightmare. In a weird way, I thought holding on to him would help me hold on to you." She looked down at the stem, now entwined with her fingers and said, "I missed you. I decided to try to have another baby to make things better, but it didn't work. I guess when they did the procedure on me, they messed stuff up. When I realized I was never going to have a baby, and

Ambrose was never going to be anything other than a psycho, I finally let go—"

The door behind them creaked open, interrupting them. Brad appeared wearing a bright pink bandana tied into a headband. "Yo, Pete, did you decide on the elevator yet?"

"Huh?" Peter looked behind him, feeling bothered by his inconvenient presence. "Um, I ordered it yesterday. It should be a few weeks before the installation crew comes."

"That long yet?"

"Yeah. Why?"

"I was just wondering about that south wall." Brad's head tilted in that direction. "If you were going to do the elevator there and what the dimensions are so I can plot out the layout for the new rooms."

"I wouldn't do any renovations on that end until we have construction on the elevator done."

"For sure, man." Brad nodded, appearing to notice Exa for the first time and he added, "I'm sorry, I didn't mean to intrude."

"No, you're cool," Peter said. "Anything else?"

"I'm good."

"You guys can go to lunch. If you want to go to the coffee shop and just charge it, I'll buy today," Peter offered.

"That sounds great. Thanks, man." Brad closed the door and disappeared back inside.

Exa smirked. "Where'd you find muscles?"

Peter immediately closed his eyes, trying to erase the image of Brad from his brain. "Don't call him that."

"Did you see his arms?" Exa made a large circle with her fingers. "Those were huge."

"I didn't notice," Peter grumbled.

She smiled, catching onto Peter's avoidance. "Okay, I get it. I didn't know I wasn't supposed to bring it up. What did he do to you?"

Peter rolled his eyes. "He's Gwen's fiancé."

"Gwen . . ." Her brows raised from her fond remembrance. "Your Gwen?"

"She's not my Gwen."

"Your friend who always came to your concerts. She's engaged to one of your crew?" Her lower lip pulled forward, while she bobbed her head in amusement. "That's an interesting twist."

"She was engaged first, then she asked me to hire him. I thought it would only last a couple days and I could find a reason to let him go, but unfortunately, he's good at his job." Peter shook his head in disgust.

Exa laughed so hard by his obvious envy, it made him chuckle a little. After the laughter died down, she continued in a somber tone, "So, here's a serious question for you."

"What?"

"Does she know how you feel?"

He furrowed his eyebrows. "No. I mean, there's nothing to know."

"Pe ta dear, do really you believe that?"

"Of course I believe it," he stubbornly insisted. "She's Gwen. We're friends."

"But does she know that you have *feelings* for her?"

"I don't . . ." He vigorously shook his head, but then Exa trapped his eyes, and although he tried to avoid them, he immediately knew she was right. Feeling defeated, he defended, "What would it matter? Her mind's made up."

She playfully bumped his arm with her elbow. "If I teach you anything in life, let it be that when it comes to a woman, her mind is *never* made up."

"What are you saying?" Peter squinted in confusion.

"I'm saying, she made her mind up based on the information present to her at *that time.* Things change, and if she were to be offered *new* information, she may change her mind."

"I'm not going to butt in, if that's what you think. She's happy."

"I'm not saying anything. I'm just wondering what would happen if she knew some new information."

Peter frowned. "She would never go with me. Look at Brad. He's a freaking model for Meat Head Gym Incorporated, complete with a spray tan. Me, I can't even walk across the room without wobbling."

"Those are superficial things outside the boundaries of love."

"I think we need to stop this stupid conversation." Peter looked around, making sure no one was around to accidentally overhear.

"I don't." She placed her arm on his forearm briefly. "Life's so short, and you don't get any do-overs. The last thing you want to do is let someone like Gwen go off without you, and not ever let her know she had another option."

Peter swallowed hard then whispered, "I can't go there." He pushed the conversation from his mind, redirecting his thoughts back towards the original conversation. "I seriously don't want to talk about Brad or Gwen. I want to know about what happened to me."

Exa shrugged like she couldn't go back to the previous conversation. "There really isn't much more to tell."

"Yes, there is. I want to know when you *knew*."

"Officially, I knew moments before you did. A private investigator came to my house that morning. He had way too many questions, and I knew instantly what he was researching. Did you know about him?"

"I just found out about that, too. My dad kept it a secret. But that's not what I meant. I meant unofficially, when did you know?"

She nervously tugged a piece of her hair, sweeping it back from her face. "Do you remember when you were little and you came over and played Pachelbel from memory without hearing it?"

He stared off, pulling his memory up and then he quietly said, "Yeah."

"You played a variation in the piece. It's a little faster tempo in the beginning that's not original to the song. It's my style variation."

"Now that I think about it—" he tilted his head thoughtfully and said "—you do have your own variation to that piece."

"How would you know that? Even if you heard the song before, you would have never heard that variation. It's *my* style variation. It was in that moment that I was convicted in my heart we had a connection— but my brain couldn't conceive it."

"I remember you wigging out and practically kicking us out after that."

"I think your mom just thought I was crazy, but she had no idea what had really just happened. I spent a few weeks researching, and that only confirmed my previous knowledge that babies absorbed music in the womb. There was only one kid I could ever justify in my mind who would have had the opportunity to learn that variation."

Peter's mouth fell open. "You knew back then? That was, like, the third time we met."

"Like I said, officially no, but in my heart, I knew something was off, or should I say on, but my brain wouldn't believe it. I knew I felt a pull towards you. When we were together, I felt my heart synced to an inner peace I had been missing."

"I think I feel that way too, but I always thought it was the music that was our bond."

"Maybe it is. The fact that our biology would be so strong that we both feel it— it's unfathomable really. But when I looked closer, I saw clues further tying us together. That's why I called your mom back and offered to keep seeing you. I had to know you."

"What other clues did you see?"

"You have my eyes."

Peter looked into Exa's sapphire eyes. "Lots of people have blue eyes."

"When I found out your birthday. That ripped a hole in my heart. It made me sick, physically ill for days. Then there's this." Exa pulled out her phone from her purse and flipped through the apps until she found her pictures. After swiping away most of the beginning ones, she stopped on one. She held her phone up for Peter to see a picture of a middle-aged man with sandy blond hair blowing in the wind as he stood on a boat, holding a mixed drink of some sort. "It's Ambrose," she said flatly. "Look at him."

He grabbed the phone from her hands, holding it just inches from his face. He had never met him or even seen a picture of him, but now, as he searched for the signs of himself, he saw them in Ambrose. Ambrose had the same overbite in his smile that Peter did. Their eyebrow lines followed the same pattern, as well as the shape to his face. They had the same up-turned nose. With the exception of Exa's eyes, Peter was a copy of Ambrose. He pushed the phone back towards her. "That's messed up."

"It's a pretty good confirmation of genetics. There are little things too. Like how when you think really hard you clench your teeth and it makes your cheeks twitch. Who would think that was genetic? But Ambrose does that too."

"Does he know about me?" Peter wrapped his arms around his elbows and leaned forward. The breeze outside had picked up, and in the distance steel gray clouds were starting to roll over the sky.

"No, I haven't really been honest with him either." She looked down. "It would be an impossible conversation."

"I guess it really doesn't matter. If you say he's a terrible person, I don't really need a person like that in my life."

"That might not be the best position for you to take." When she looked at Peter, her eyes filled with so much fear that it scared him.

"What do you mean?"

"I know about your operation. I talked to your mom. I was ready to do it tomorrow, but—"

"But what?" Peter interrupted, filling his chest instantly fill with rage. "How can there be a 'but'?"

"I'm not the O."

"Huh?"

"I'm not the O. My blood type is A-positive."

CHAPTER SEVEN

"You sold tickets for a grand each!" Peter scolded Gwen, who ducked behind the counter at the coffee shop.

"It's for charity. I decided to make all the money for the show tonight go towards the school renovations."

"That's robbery. Who would even pay that much?" He asked as he approached the counter.

"A lot of people."

"Nobody's gonna pay that."

"We sold out." Gwen grinned smugly.

"How?"

"Paul said we could only sell ninety tickets because of the fire code, so I wanted to make the show worth your while. Everyone knows you canceled your big tour, so these tickets were a rare commodity. It was easy to sell them." She explained as she walked out from behind the counter with a box of napkins, heading to a table by the window.

He pushed his lower jaw forward and stewed before saying, "I really didn't want this to be a big deal."

"But it is! Your fans are excited to see you play again." She flashed an excited look toward him, as she continued to breeze through her chores and opened the napkin dispenser on the table, filling it with new napkins.

"You could've told me a little sooner than two hours before the show starts."

"Sorry." She scrunched her nose.

"Too late now." Peter moved towards the bookcase next to the table she was cleaning. Running his hands over the book binds, he searched for something to catch his eye, and changed the subject, "So, who was that guy here talking to you when I walked in?"

Gwen closed the dispenser and pushed it back against the wall. "That was Hal, my insurance man."

Peter looked carefully at her before speaking, "Do you need health insurance? We could probably work something out here."

"No, I'm actually still on my mom's plan for the time being. She has really good stuff through her job at the post office." Gwen wiped dried ketchup off the wall with a rag. Now it was her turn to change the subject. "How anyone gets ketchup all the way up here is beyond me."

"It's pretty gross cleaning this place. Is it too much work for you? I can always look at adding an extra cleaning person."

"No, it's not too much work. Just gross."

"So," Peter reverted to the previous topic, "if you have health insurance through your mom, what was that dude doing here?"

Gwen flashed an irritated look at Peter. "Just 'cause you want to know?"

"I don't mean to be nosey. It just looked like a serious conversation." He neatly stacked up the books on the shelf, trying to act casual.

"If you must know, I was adding a life-insurance policy." She leaned over on the booth bench and tucked her head under the table, reaching down to pick up a crumpled napkin.

"Life insurance. For what?"

She glared at him. "For the obvious."

"What obvious?"

"It's just to have some money for my family for when something happens. Brad thought it was a good idea. So that my mom doesn't get stuck with a bunch of bills. She doesn't have anyone else to help her. It's always been only the two of us."

"I guess that makes sense," Peter said softly, but then added, "I hope you know if anything happens to you and your mom isn't okay, I would help her."

Gwen's lips turned up slightly. "I know. This is just, you know— in case. What are you doing here now anyway? Shouldn't you be getting ready?"

"I'm here because I have a surprise for you, but now I don't know if you deserve it." Peter playfully glared at her, who batted her eyelashes back innocently towards him.

"I love surprises."

"I know." He sighed, giving into her. "Follow me outside," he said. Gwen eagerly hopped down from the booth and was fast on his heels out the door where they found Brad outside, standing in front of his truck. In the truck bed was a large object concealed by a blanket. Gwen ran to it.

"Ooo, what is it?" She grabbed the edge of the blanket, trying to peek under it.

Peter pushed her hand away. "Not so fast. I want to say something first."

Gwen's gaze bounced from Brad to Peter. Peter continued, "I wasn't into this grand-opening thing you wanted to do, but then I had a thought: if we are gonna do this, we need to do it right. So." Peter pulled the blanket from the object, revealing a large sign that said, "Gwen's Gourmet Grind."

Gwen's face lit up like the north star on a cloudless night. "Is this for the outside? Are you renaming the place?"

"I am. It's your shop. Tonight's the grand reopening, so, I thought we should make it a rebranding, too."

"I absolutely love it," Gwen squealed.

"Brad's going to install it so it's ready to go for tonight."

Brad looked at Gwen. "Before I do, I wanted to get your picture in front of it."

"Sure," she said, her smile was so large it filled her whole face. Brad took his phone out of his pocket, handing it to Peter.

"Do you mind? I'd like to be in it too," Brad said.

Peter swallowed, filling that stupid knot in the pit of his stomach appear again. "Sure, that's no problem." He held the phone up while the couple positioned themselves in front of the sign with their arms wrapped around each other. As Peter watched them get cozy, he felt himself wishing he was the one standing next to Gwen. Quickly pushing that thought as far from his mind as he could, he snapped the photo, and handed the phone back. He wasn't sure why, but he all the sudden felt like he needed to take a break to be alone. He excused himself, citing a need to prepare for the show, and left them alone to celebrate.

AN HOUR LATER, BRAD HAD THE SIGN UP AND GWEN WAS BUSY STOCKING coffee cups with the new logo on them that Peter had stashed for tonight. Paul had arrived to move in a keyboard. The film crew was also there setting up equipment. The doors had been locked early and were not going to be opened until fifteen minutes before the show.

A loud banging on the door caught Peter's attention. Paul answered it, and after seeing who it was, he opened the door to let Exa inside.

"Are you early for the show?" Paul asked. Peter called out, "No, I asked her to stop by."

"Oh, are you going to play tonight too?" Gwen asked, her voice starting to pitch higher with excitement.

"No, I'm not playing," Exa said.

"Guys, she's just here to see me." Peter waved at her. "Come on back. I have a little space set up in the roasting room." He led the way back through the kitchen and up a couple steps to a back room that held the roaster and extra storage. "I need to get changed anyway." He pulled his duffle bag out from under a table and dug through it.

"Looks like you're dressing pretty casual tonight."

"I didn't think it was going to be a big deal, but I guess Gwen raised a lot of money." He explained as he pulled out a crumbled, black T-shirt.

Exa watched as he slipped it on, but she furrowed her brow and asked, "Do you think you could add a sport coat or something over it?" She tilted her head, examining him. "You look like a homeless kid who wandered into a coffee shop."

"I can have my mom bring a jacket for me if you think it will be better."

"I do."

He grabbed his phone, texted his mom, and set his phone back on the table. Then he looked back at her and said, "So, this is awkward, but I have to ask you."

"What?"

"Ambrose. I don't even know how to find him. What's his real last name?"

"Why?" Exa nervously shifted her feet.

"Because you said you're not the O. Nothing has changed on my end. I'm still on a timeline." He grinned anxiously, desperate to try to keep the conversation light.

She folded her arms across her chest, sending a signal to Peter that she was going to be stubborn about this. "I don't think that's a good idea. For you to talk to him, I mean."

Peter's eyebrows arched in urgency. "It's the only idea I have left. Good idea or bad idea, I have to go with it."

"No, it's not a bad idea. It's a terrible idea."

Peter's jaw dropped slightly before he said, "Did you hear me? I'm out of options. I need a kidney."

"I heard you. I know you need a kidney, but contacting Ambrose is not an option."

Peter's voice raised, now expressing his total disbelief. "Not an option? Exa! If I don't get a kidney, I'm going to die. How can contacting Ambrose be worse than death?"

She pursed her lips and then spoke, "Pe ta, I can't explain it. I want you to have that kidney more than anything, but Ambrose is not the guy to ask."

"He's the only one left! It's not a choice." He rubbed his finger joints as he felt them tensing up from the frustration of how stubborn Exa could be.

Exa motioned to the only chair in the room. "You're gonna wanna sit down for this."

Peter diligently sat, not wanting to give her any excuse to withhold information from him. He did his best to give her a guilty stare while he waited for her to talk.

"You're not going to like what I have to say."

"Do I ever lately?"

"Ambrose, he's not your typical guy. He's mean, he's vengeful."

Peter interrupted, "I get it. He's a jerk, but I don't care. It's not like his personality is attached to his kidney. It won't transplant into me."

"No, he's not a jerk. I mean, he's a jerk, but that's not all. Do you know what a narcissist is?"

"Like someone who's obsessed with themselves?"

"I think that's sort of a more relaxed definition of it. But Ambrose, he's a classic textbook narcissist. He will lie and cheat and plan revenge."

"Again, I don't care. That's not going to be attached to his kidney."

"The thing is, he hates me. And he will hate you because you're you," her voice trailed off.

Peter's face remained unchanged, "So what?"

"He won't do it. He won't give you a kidney. He's an evil man who will do everything to make me sad. If I tell him what I want, he does the opposite just to put me in my place. He'll never accept that you are alive. Worse, he will take pleasure in the fact that he has the control to take you away from me," her words rattled out like she was trying to get hot coal out of her mouth.

Peter squinted his eyes in disbelief. "How could he not, if he knew he was my last resort?"

She placed a hand on his shoulder. "Take my advice. Stay away from him. I know he is your last resort, but it's not worth it. He will never help you, and only make what life you have left miserable. He's not capable of caring for anyone."

"So you're saying it's better for me to die slowly, than to try to live?" Peter's mouth was dry. He looked around for his water bottle. Nothing.

"I'm saying you have a wonderful family, and friends who love you. Spend what time you have with them. Live your life to the fullest every day. Live it completely. And don't dwell on Ambrose. You should be spending your energy on that other person we talked about."

Peter scowled. "What are you talking about?"

"I'm talking about that girl out there." She pointed out the door. "That's *your* girl, and even if you are the last one to see it, you'd better do something fast, or she's gonna marry muscles, and it will haunt you for the rest of your life."

"Stop talking about Gwen. She's made a choice already. Right now, I need a kidney, so I need Ambrose."

"I'm not talking about Ambrose anymore because he's not worth even my breath and I honestly don't want to make you more upset." She turned on her heel, walking towards the door. Once in the doorway, she looked back and added, "This hurts me more than it hurts you and I know it's killing you, but please just promise me to live your life and stay away from him."

Peter grimaced. "I can promise to live my life, but I can't promise to stay away from him."

"Very well then. I warned you." She narrowed her eyes, and then left.

Peter rubbed his chin. Confused, he pushed the conversation from his mind. He had to get ready. Digging through his duffle bag some more, he pulled out some deodorant, pulled the cap off, and was applying it when he heard, "Hey, Pete."

Gwen was standing in the door and holding her usual preconcert bouquet of purple lilies. Exchanging purple lilies was a tradition they had gotten into ever since their first meeting when Peter gave her some lilies before his show. He reached out and took the flowers. He let his eyes pace over her face while his voice lightly retraced a recent quote, "Like a lily among the thorns, so is my darling among the maidens."

"That's pretty." Her head tilted to the side, while she let it sink it. "Is that Shakespeare?"

"No, it's the Bible." Peter said as he lowered his eyes, feeling slightly shy around her, remembering what Exa had just told him. Then trying to tease her, he added, "You should read more."

"I would rather go to the movie."

"I'm not sure that's in theatres." He set the flowers carefully on the table. "I was beginning to think you forgot."

"No, I didn't forget. It's just hard to find the right kind of lily."

"I know, I have thought many times we should switch to roses or carnations because you can find those anywhere."

"That's half the fun of it. I always get a rush wondering where I will find them." She smiled, and the dimple on her chin peeked out. Peter stared at it. She was so familiar to him. Everything about her was something he knew and had memorized: from the way her hair curled naturally but frizzed when it was humid; from her freckles on her nose that stayed hidden in the winter, but would come out with the first sunny day in the spring; the way she sang to herself when she got engrossed in cleaning, and the way she then would get embarrassed when she realized someone was listening. *I know you better than anyone. You're my Gwen.*

"I wanted to thank you for tonight. For letting me do this even though you didn't want to, and for the sign with the new name. That's really special." She beamed with gratitude.

Peter could feel his cheeks pinken. "Don't mention it. The pleasure's all mine."

"Well I did, but I guess I should let you finish getting ready. The doors are about to open." Gwen backed toward the door of the tiny room.

"Wait!" Peter hadn't planned on calling out to her, but something in his chest had suddenly sprung to life.

"Hmm." She glanced back super quick, waiting for the rest of his comment.

"It's just." Peter rubbed his thumb joint, then lost his nerve. "Nothing."

"No, what's up?" Gwen turned her body this time, and now face him.

"It's just, ahh, I can't. Never mind." Peter could hear all the noise outside the room and the timing was just so wrong for this conversation, but then Exa's words echoed in his ears . . . *Promise me to live your life to the fullest.*

"No, you can tell me." Gwen took a step closer to him, touching his arm out of concern. "Do you feel okay?"

He could smell the amber in her perfume, and it made him want to step even closer to her. It caused a deep unsettling in his gut that made him blurt out, "I feel fine except for the fact that I don't."

"Do you need something?" Gwen had a worried look on her face.

Peter forced himself to look at her. *Yeah, you.* But he froze, locked on her gaze. *I don't know why I'm not okay with you being happy with him. I'm dying inside.* "Gwen, I need to know."

"What?"

He licked his lips, then asked, "Would it have mattered if I would've asked first?"

Gwen swallowed, her eyes still entwined with his were now widening, but instead of filling with affection, they quickly put up a shield. Peter saw her truth manifest in her eyes. It made him want to dry heave but luckily, she broke his eye contact, turning away.

"You hoo. There you are." Anne burst through the door, holding a hanger with a jacket covered in plastic wrap, fresh from the dry cleaners. "I barely made it through that crowd. It's so exciting to see all the people here," her voice trailed off when she saw the expression on Peter's face. Her eyes shifted to Gwen's face and then back to Peter's. "Am I interrupting something?"

Peter cleared his throat. "No, Gwen was just leaving." He glared at Gwen, daring her to leave. Gwen's eyes sparkled from a moisture that wasn't there before. She left and she softly whispered, "Good luck tonight, Pete. I love you." Her words came out like a stone. Peter knew that the love she spoke of would never be anything other than friendship.

CHAPTER EIGHT

*P*eter hunched over his keyboard in the corner of the coffee shop. A microphone stand towered in front of him. The intimacy of the audience--being small and close--was comfortable, yet there was an element of invasiveness he wasn't used to. He could see all the faces in the crowd, including the one face he wanted to erase—Gwen. Worse yet, it looked like she had been crying.

"Good evening," he spoke over the applause, and then waited for it to die out. "I'm excited to be with you tonight, and thanks for coming out to support our charity."

A few people in the back of the room were chatting, and it was distracting. Peter pulled the mic stand closer to make it louder. "So, this coffee house gig thing is new to me, and I wanted to keep it casual. I'll play some of my sonatas, but I thought it would be cool to play some modern music too. I was hoping you guys could help me. Do you think you could do that?"

Applause filled the room and a few people whistled. "That's great. So, I'm doing open requests, but to keep it organized so you're not all shouting, we have a request book right here. Just come over and write down what you want to hear--sort of like karaoke. And if you haven't grabbed a coffee yet, please go ahead. We also have wine available since it's a special occasion. It's all free tonight." Cheering burst out.

"I wanted to start off with something sort of special. Anyone who knows me knows that my mom and I are close." Peter surfed the crowd for his mom, and when he found her she was blushing.

"My mom used to sing to me when I was little. I was a terrible sleeper, so long before I found piano, my memories of music were my mom singing me to sleep *several* times a night. I want to do this for her. She's a fan of many people, but Stevie Nicks was one I heard a lot of, and to this day, I always think of her." Peter's lips curved into a mischievous smile. "Better yet, she's gonna *kill* me, but I was hoping you all could help me get her to come sit by me for this one and encourage her to sing."

The crowd cheered again. Anne shook her head and tried to back up against the wall, but the insistent crowd pushed her forward. She covered her face with her hands and embarrassedly dragged her feet until she was upfront, and sat on the stool next to Peter, who planted the mic stand in front of her, pushing it shorter. Her face was a shade of red so deep you could see purple undertones.

"Come on, Mom. In all the years I've been doing this, I've never called you up on stage. It's about time."

The crowd started chanting, "Sing. Sing. Sing." Peter saw his brothers, Tane and Shiloh, and his dad in the corner--all of them laughing. Anne playfully shook a fist at Peter. He took that as a yes and played the first chords to "Landslide," and the crowd hushed.

At first, Anne was squeaky, which was understandable, but after she warmed up, she found her cue. She kept her eyes locked on Peter's. His presence carried her through the rush she felt. Then it was over. Thomas had made his way over and pulled Anne off stage, hugging her while they laughed like kids.

"Thanks, Mom," Peter called after her. "Okay, so next, I want to play a song from my new album, called, 'Identity.'" He sat at the keyboard and played. The first segment of his performance breezed by, and he was exhilarated. "Alright everyone, I'm going to take five, but before I do, I need to thank someone who made tonight possible." He held his hand graciously out toward Gwen. "Gwen has been my friend for years, and now she is managing this place for me and it's been amazing having her here. She also makes the best cheesecake, which is going to be available here shortly for you all to try. Please help me thank her."

Even from all the way across the room, Gwen's eyes were able to meet Peter's. She smiled like she appreciated the comment, but she held his gaze so long, Peter was able to detect a wistfulness, making him curious because her expression didn't exude the joy of the moment.

The crowd started to disperse and got chatty. Paul interrupted Peter's eye lock with Gwen by offering him a bottle of water. "You look like you're having fun."

"I'm enjoying it. Did Exa leave? I was going to pull her up next."

"No, she's still here. You know who else is here?"

"Who?"

"Mrs. Polly, your old music teacher."

"Really? I can't believe she'd pay that much money to see me. You should totally find her and send her over here."

"Okay, I'll try." Paul bobbed his head and wove back into the crowd.

A fast five later, Peter sat back at the piano with Mrs. Polly on his side. The duo played several of the requests together. They belted lyrics out as they bobbed their heads to the different melodies. The energy in the room was that of close friends and family--all who loved him.

As the crowd shifted around, he recognized many people, including the nurse who did his dialysis at the hospital. That stung. He wanted to forget about his stupid kidney for one night. He quickly looked away from her. Peter took a swig from his water bottle, leaned into the mic and said, "This next song's another one from my first album, but I still like it, so let's do it. Ruby in the Water."

Everyone cheered.

He played the first chords and again he felt his eyes gravitate to find Gwen. This time she was with Brad. She was facing Peter, watching the show but Brad was behind her, his arms wrapped around her waist. It was obvious Gwen saw Peter looking at her, and she flashed him a giant smile and gave him a thumbs up.

Peter played, watching Gwen with Brad. Their embrace hit him like a boulder, and suddenly he realized what a blind fool he'd always been. He froze, forgetting about everyone there except for Gwen. He looked daggers at her. People whispered. Gwen blushed and looked away, but Peter continued to be frozen on her. Then he grabbed the mic and said, "Let's take five." When he released the mic stand, it squealed as it swung back to an upright position.

He bee-lined to the back room, ignoring the people talking to him on the way. *That,* the closeness of his audience--them being close enough to touch him--was not something he was used to. He was alone for only a moment when his dad walked into the room. "Did you guys flip a coin to see who had to come in here?" Peter asked sarcastically.

Thomas didn't move. "No."

"I messed up. I forgot the chords and it freaked me out. That's never happened before." Peter spouted out the first excuse he could come up with, but then he was distracted because he saw Gwen's lilies lying on the table. They were starting to wilt from lack of water. He picked them up, rubbing one of the velvety petals with his thumb.

"Sure," Thomas said. "Just making sure you're feeling okay. We didn't want a repeat of the last performance."

"No, I think I'm good there. I'm actually feeling pretty strong physically."

"And what about that other stuff--"

"TOM!" A shrill came from somewhere. "Come quick! Tom, where are you?" Anne was screaming. Peter and Thomas both scrambled through the door. Thomas leaped out front, leaving Peter to wobble slower to see the crowd had all fanned themselves along the outside walls of the room, allowing the center of the floor to be open and clear except for three people. One of them was Anne, who now had her phone to her ear, and Brad, who was kneeling, hunched over someone.

"It's Gwen," Anne said. "She collapsed. I'm calling an ambulance."

"No, don't bother. It's faster if we take her," Thomas said.

Peter hugged the wall behind him as he watched Brad scoop up Gwen and they all ran out the door.

CHAPTER NINE

*H*ours after the concert, Peter's cell phone vibrated. He was alone at the coffee shop. Still.

"Dad," Peter answered when he saw the caller I.D.

"She's okay. False alarm."

Peter sighed, like he was finally able to breathe.

"She was dehydrated, and low on potassium and magnesium. We're giving her some IV's, but she'll be fine."

"Did you see her chart?"

"I did. Why?"

"Did you see it?"

"See what?"

"The cancer."

Thomas was quiet. "Dad," Peter pressed.

"You know I can't say. It's a confidentiality thing."

"I know it's there."

"Well then, you probably know what Gwen wants you to know."

"That's bull! I have a right to know. How bad is it?"

Thomas was silent again.

"Dad!"

"I'm sorry. These things have a way of working themselves out, but for now I think you know what you need to know."

"Well, that's great. Thanks for nothing." Peter ended the call, flipped his phone down on the counter in front of him, and squeezed his hands into fists.

The next day, Peter arrived at the hospital for dialysis, but he also had another mission. Carrying a fresh bouquet of purple lilies tucked in his arm, he sped past the floor map because he had the halls of this placed memorized. He knew she would be on the third floor. He arrived in the elevator and walked to the nurses' station.

"Excuse me, mam," he said to a charge nurse.

She had a pleasant smile on her face when she asked, "Hello, how can I help you?"

"Can you please tell me what room Gweneviere Davis is in?"

"Yes, certainly." She looked down at the computer and then frowned. "There is a no-visitors request for that patient. It says we can give updates on how she's doing, but unless you are on the list of family, you can't see her."

"Oh, I'm sure I'm on the list. Peter Arnold."

She looked at the list and then shook her head. "No, sorry."

"Hum, that has to be a mistake. I'll call her mom to fix it." Peter pulled out his cell, calling Olivia.

"Hello," Olivia picked up the phone.

"Hey, Olivia, it's Peter."

"Hi Pete. How are you?" Her voice was welcoming.

"I'm okay. I'm actually waiting out here at the nurses' station. My name wasn't put on the list to see Gwen, so they are holding me hostage. Can you come down here to add me?"

There was a pause, and then Olivia said, "Can you hold on a minute? Brad's here."

"Okay . . ." Peter heard muffled voices.

"Yo, Pete," Brad said.

"Hey. There's been a misunderstanding with the visitor list. Can you add me to the list? I have some flowers for Gwen. I won't stay long. I actually have dialysis, but I wanted to say hello."

"Yeah, about that."

"About what?"

"I'm sorry, man. But, Gwen's tired right now. We want to limit her company to people who are just family. It wasn't an accident your name was left off."

"What?" Peter's brows pulled to the ceiling in shock. "That's messed up."

"I'm sorry you feel that way, bro. But we feel it's what is best."

"Who's 'we'? Did you ask Gwen? Can I talk to her?"

"No, she's resting. I'm sorry, but I need to go. I'll let her know you called." The phone went silent. Peter stared down the hallway, unable to pass the nurses' station. He wanted to call out, "Gwen! I'm here. Your boyfriend's a douche!" But he didn't, instead he huffed and in a frustrated tone asked, "Can you just make sure she gets these?" He held up the flowers, handing them over to the nurse and then went to dialysis.

THE NEXT MORNING, PETER ARRIVED AT THE SCHOOL TO MAKE SURE HIS crew was working while Brad was absent. He stepped into the lobby and was surprised to find Olivia was there hurriedly packing.

"Hey." Peter stood in the entryway, confused at the scene.

Olivia looked up. "Hi, I'm just getting Gwen's stuff. The door was open. I hope that's okay I came in."

"That's fine." Peter took a few steps closer, ready to assist her. "Does she have to stay in the hospital much longer?"

Olivia folded Gwen's Elvis blanket and said, "No, she's getting out this morning as soon as the doctor comes to discharge her."

"My dad said something about how they wouldn't keep her long. Hey —" he motioned to her in an inviting way, "—did you need a place to stay while you're here? I can't believe I didn't mention it, but you're welcome to stay here too."

"I'm going home today." She kept her eyes low, avoiding him. "I was hoping Brad could talk to you before now, but I see you don't know, do you?"

"Know what?"

"We are taking Gwen home." She looked up briefly and Peter could tell there was a guilt in her eyes, but she didn't linger at all and quickly turned back, stacking Gwen's pillows, and further explained, "She feels awful about the coffee shop, but Brad thought it was getting to be too much for her and that's why she got so run down. He wants her to take the summer off and focus on planning the wedding."

"No." Peter was confused a took another step closer. "Gwen never said a word, but then again," he lowered his voice in frustration, "I haven't been able to talk to her."

"She doesn't want you to be mad at her," Olivia said softly, then added, "Brad wanted to take care of everything for her."

"No, that's cool," Peter said slowly as he tried to figure out why it seemed like Gwen was being kept from him. He was also concerned about her and didn't want her to be overwhelmed so he added, "I wouldn't want her to keep working if she doesn't feel up to it. I know what it's like to be sick. Tell her not to worry about the coffee shop."

Olivia stood up straight, brushing her hands off on her jeans. "Thanks. It's so nice you do understand."

"Maybe I'll come up after I'm done here so I can say goodbye and make sure she knows not to worry about the coffee shop. Do you think that would be okay?"

"Um, you could try." Olivia grabbed the duffle bag, hanging it on her shoulder, then retrieved the stack of pillows and blankets.

"Alright, tell Gwen I'll be up in a few minutes." He held his hands out, ready to assist. "Do you need help carrying this stuff out?"

"I'm okay." She inched toward the door. "I already loaded the heavy one in the car. This was the last of it."

"See you in a bit." He started to wave, but then remembered something and said, "Can you make sure to add me to the visitors' list?"

"Okay. Will do." Olivia smiled timidly at him before closing the door behind her.

Once she was gone, Peter turned to Gwen's now empty cot. *Might as well just move this out of the way now that it's going to be empty.* He reached underneath the cot to find the latch to make it fold in half. He heard a click, then folded it and latched it shut. He pivoted it out of the way to set it against the wall and his foot kicked an envelope. *Olivia must have overlooked this.* He picked it up and was going to put it under his arm when he recognized it. It was the large manila envelope Gwen had gotten at the coffee shop. The one her insurance guy left her. *Don't look at it. It's private.* Gwen's words about how she wanted to have funds to care for her mom if anything happened to her rung in his head. *It's none of my business.* Peter tried to talk himself out of opening it, but his curiosity got the best of him.

He pulled the paper stack out of the envelope, peeking at the first page, which was the summary page. *TWO MILLION DOLLARS!* He yanked out the stack of papers and scanned the page, letting his eyes read the conditions of payment until he got to the bottom where it said beneficiary: Brad Dillard was next to the primary beneficiary line and there was no secondary one. Peter frantically flipped through the stack of pages, looking for another page that would declare Olivia to have some ownership of the funds, but there was nothing. His gut hardened. He already knew the answer and it was the answer he was afraid of since he had met Brad. *Brad was using Gwen.*

Not wasting a hot second, Peter sped to the hospital, hoping to catch Gwen before she left. Once inside the hospital, he bolted toward her room, running into Brad as he was coming out of the elevator. Brad shifted his shoulders toward Peter, like he was ready to have a friendly conversation and asked, "Hey, Pete, what's happening?"

Peter couldn't even fake nice. He was so fuming mad when he asked, "Where's Gwen?"

"Oh yeah." He flashed a disappointed look toward Peter and said, "Sorry, we missed you but she's on her way home. Her mom just left with her." Peter's eye's narrowed, and he felt his heart pound against his rib cage while he continued to listen to Brad say, "I was gonna come talk to you about handing in my notice, and I have to get some of my stuff, too."

Peter stood stunned. It was so obvious that Brad was purposely trying to keep him from seeing Gwen. He knew better than to argue with someone as stupid as Brad but didn't want to let him completely off the hook so he said, "Olivia must have been running because I just saw her twenty minutes ago at the school. What's the rush?"

"No rush. Gwen's just tired and wants to get home."

"I see." Peter's eyes narrowed even more while he soaked up Brad's lies.

"So, are we cool with the school gig? You know I can't stay."

"Um, yeah." *I never wanted you around in the first place.*

"Cool, so I'll just text you an address to send my last paycheck to."

"Okay."

"Sweet, I'll tell Gwen you stopped by, and I'll see you around, Pete." Brad shoved his hand out for a handshake, flashing his big, dumb smile.

"Bye," Peter said under his breath, refusing to even look at Brad's extended hand. He was relieved to see Brad go, but there was a grinding feeling in his gut, screaming at him that he didn't even know the worst of Brad.

After he watched Brad dash out the back corridor, Peter quickly took his phone out to text Gwen, but he wasn't surprised when Gwen didn't reply. He tried to brush it off, saying she was resting but after many unanswered texts and a few days had past, Peter lost his patience and once again called Olivia.

"Hi," Olivia said.

"Hey, it's Peter."

"Hey," her voice held an air of hesitation when she asked, "How are you?"

"I'm okay," Peter spoke quickly, ready to get to the point of the call. "I've been trying to get ahold of Gwen, but she doesn't text me back. Did she get a new number or something?"

Silence.

"Olivia?"

"Yeah . . . I should have you talk to Brad."

"I don't want to talk to Brad," he said sternly. "I called you."

"I know you mean well." Her voice was so soft, it made Peter think she was trying to speak in secret. "I think it's better if you maybe not push the issue."

"The issue? I can't get ahold of my best friend who has cancer. That's sort of a big deal."

"Gwen's fine. Really. You don't have to worry about her health."

"Okay . . . then can I get a number where I can get ahold of her at?"

Olivia sighed, sounding conflicted. "Between you and I, I don't think you should contact her."

"Why not?" Peter asked, but he already knew the answer.

"Well," her voice was down to a whisper, confirming that she was in fact, trying to hide the conversation. "Brad got jealous of your friendship while he was there. It's minor really. I'm sure after he gets used to being back home, he'll get over it."

"So, I can't talk to Gwen? Does Gwen know that? Is that why she hasn't replied to any of my texts?"

"I think Brad asked her not to talk to you."

"Why?"

"To be truthful," her voice was still so hushed, it was hard to hear. "I think it has something to do with why Gwen was crying at the concert."

Peter's air got trapped in his throat when he thought about the conversation, he had that night with Gwen. "You know about that?"

"Sort of . . ."

"What do you know?"

"I know Gwen had a really hard time with your conversation."

"Does Brad know?"

"Brad and Gwen are getting married. I don't think they keep secrets."

"They don't keep secrets but yet, Brad doesn't want me to talk to Gwen?"

"I think it's just temporary."

Olivia spoke in a manner that tried to smooth over the comment, but Peter cut her off, and said, "Well, can you give them each a message for me?"

"Sure."

"Tell Gwen that I called to see how she was. And tell Brad I know what he's up to, and I refuse to let him get away with it!" Peter hung up his phone and hurled it at the wall, letting his now empty fists ball. *I just can't stand that guy!*

CHAPTER TEN

"*E*xa! Let me in. Answer the door!" Peter pounded his fist on her front door. The sky was overcast with dark, ugly, gray clouds that showed no sign of mercy, pouring rain on him.

Exa swung the front door open. Peter didn't wait to be invited inside and water dripped from every surface of his body as he trudged through the front door.

"Wait here; I'll grab a towel." She disappeared into the adjacent bathroom, returning with a white shower towel. "I'd offer you something dry to put on," she offered a teasing smile, "but I don't have anything in your size."

"Yah, I don't wear black dresses." Peter wiped his face off, blinking his eyes to get them to focus.

"So, what's going on, Pe ta?" She motioned to the back of the house where the kitchen was. "Can I make you some tea?"

"No tea." He planted his feet firmly on the floor, just a small step from her. "I just came here to get Ambrose's address."

Exa rolled her eyes. "Well, that's a waste of time. I already told you to forget about him."

"I'm not playing. I'm not a little kid. I can take care of myself and I'm not leaving until I have his address."

Exa's gaze hardened. She pulled out her phone and clicked on a social media tab. "You're lucky I remembered this. I don't keep tabs on him, but he posted this to brag about his new house."

Peter reached for her phone. "Where's the address?"

She swiped her finger up, indicating Peter needed to scroll further down to a heading that read, "The Chateau de Marquis".

"It's a picture of a castle," he said, sounding confused.

"That's his house; he bought that."

"Who buys a castle?"

"Told you he was an arrogant piece of work." She crossed her arms over her chest. "I will never defend him. You asked. Happy?"

"Not yet, but closer." Peter zoomed in on the photo, studying the real estate. It was more spread out than most pictures of castle's he'd ever seen. "Is that a moat?" Peter asked, letting his finger rest on something that looked like a giant ditch.

"That's what it looked like to me."

"Why would he need a moat?"

"Probably to keep out all the demons who own his soul." Exa scoffed while she also reached her hand to grab the towel back from Peter and returned it to the bathroom. From the bathroom, she called out, "You might as well know his real name is Ambrose Black, but you'll know him by his stage name." She reappeared in the room. "Frankie Nevo." She flinched as she spit his name out.

Peter's jaw dropped. "The singer from Black Inferno?"

Exa nodded her head, but her face was pitched in a way that showed she was embarrassed.

"I don't get it. I saw that picture of him on your phone. He looks nothing like Frankie."

"Well, he dresses up to perform. He's always been into using heavy, ugly, stage make-up. He likes that goth look, and he dyes his hair when he performs, or wears a big wig."

Still in disbelief, Peter said, "I know who Frankie is, and to be honest, he always scared me to death. How did you guys ever end up as a couple?"

"I was young and dumb; and remember, he wasn't Frankie when I met him. Fame did a lot to destroy the likable parts of his personality. Sorry, I know it's a lot to absorb, but you wanted to know. Take the information for what it's worth. It's not too late to ignore it."

"I can't ignore it. I need him too badly to ignore it."

"I don't think it's worth your time." She shook her head, in a disapproving way. "Don't be saying I didn't warn you."

"I know." Part of him heard her warning perfectly, and it scared him, but he ignored that part because he really felt out of options. "I have to try for myself."

"Well, good luck," her words held more caution than Peter was comfortable with.

~

FIVE DAYS LATER, PETER STOOD IN THE SHADOW OF THE CHATEAU DE Marquis in Limousin, France. Maybe, it was the fact Peter knew who was living inside of it—or just the fact no one was around—but the castle emitted a creepy essence, sending chills along Peter's body.

He peered through the iron gate, looking for a way in. Leaning on his cane, he pulled his left foot, as it was dragging heavy today. A modern security system camera and keypad were attached to the gate post. Not having a better idea, Peter pushed the buzzer. A minute passed, and to his surprise the gate automatically opened. He ambled through the opened gate up the driveway which led over a little bridge crossing the moat.

He made it up the walkway to the house and knocked on the tiny door, and it opened immediately. A short, fat guy in a black suit stood there. "Can I help you?" he asked. His white hair stood up on the sides identical to how you would see a mad scientist in movies.

"I'm looking for Ambrose Black. Is this his house?" Peter shifted nervously on his feet.

"It is. Is he expecting you?" The man's voice was softer than Peter thought it should be to match his round body. He sounded smart and nervous, sort of like Rabbit from *Winnie the Pooh*.

"Not exactly." Peter's palms were sweating. "I'm a friend of his, ah, wife's . . ."

The man twisted his face into the most confusing smile Peter had ever seen. "I shall check with him first. Who shall I say you are?"

"Um, Peter. He should know."

"Very well then. Please wait here." The man shut the door. Seconds later, he reopened the door wider this time, holding his arm out to invite Peter inside. "He will see you in the library. Follow me." He waddled past the grand staircase in the entryway, into a hall, and opened the first door on the left, pausing to allow Peter to enter the room. The room reeked of dust and mildew, making his eyes itch, and his sinuses immediately filled with fluid. "Please have a seat. He shall be here shortly," the man said and then left.

Peter rubbed his itching nose, looking around the room to see a red Queen Anne couch and desk in the center. Except for stacks of bookcases along the outer walls, there was no other furniture. He could see a layer of dust film covering the couch. Not wanting to disturb it for fear that he would start his sneezing attacks, Peter remained standing, but he did take a second to hang his cane on the back of the couch.

He turned when he heard a shuffle in the doorway. Ambrose appeared, looking casual wearing jeans and a band T-shirt; his sandy blond hair was grown out to his shoulders, and he wore it straight, parted in the middle. Their eyes locked, each one daring the other to speak first. Then Ambrose said, "We finally meet." He walked farther into the room, not cracking even the slightest smile.

Peter shifted on his feet. They were tired, and he was having an impossible time standing. He wanted to sit so badly. "Do you know who I am?" he asked apprehensively. Peter could feel Ambrose's eyes staring at his knotted finger joints that curled around the top of the sofa. Growing self-conscious, He pulled them back down to his sides.

"Have a seat. You look tired," Ambrose said, as he motioned to the couch.

"I'm okay." Peter's eyes burned from the dust-coated room. He looked to the window on the wall that was between two book shelves, wishing he could open it.

"I do know who you are," Ambrose said as he continued to walk around the outskirts of the room, circling Peter the way a cat would stalk a mouse. When he got to his desk, he crossed in front and leaned against it, facing Peter. He looked older in person than he did on his Internet profiles. His wrinkles were patterned in an intriguing way—in that most people's wrinkles outlined their smile and laugh lines—but his wrinkles ironically outlined a scowl.

"I, ah, just wanted to meet you," Peter struggled to remember the words he had rehearsed.

Ambrose rested his palm on his chin, and lightly rubbed the whisker stubble that shadowed his face. "That's it?"

Peter nodded, starting to wonder if this had been a bad idea.

"Well then." Ambrose leaned over to the side of the desk, and pulled open a file drawer, revealing a mini-bar. He pulled out a bottle of caramel-colored liquid and a glass, holding it up, he asked, "Drink?"

"No thank you. I don't drink."

"Sorry, the place's a little untidy." Ambrose poured himself a drink while he talked. "I just moved in. I haven't found a housekeeper yet. You met Doc; he's the only staff I have right now. Well, him and the gardener."

"He's a doctor?"

Ambrose released a deep chuckle. "No, he's no doctor. That's what I call him because he looks like that crazy doctor from *Back to the Future*. Well, plus about fifty pounds. He has a thing for carbs though."

Peter stared blankly at Ambrose. The movie reference wasn't registering.

"Tell me you know the movie. Or was that before your time? Kids today don't know what entertainment is." Ambrose shook his head in disappointment.

"I've never seen it."

"Great movie. Worth a watch." He nodded reassuringly, but then changed the conversation. "So, are we going to beat around a bush for a couple hours while I drink by myself or are you going to tell me why you're really here?"

"Why do you think there's another reason?" Peter asked, nervously.

Locking eyes on Peter's in an unflinching manner, he said, "I know who you are, and I didn't mean Peter Arnold or Ruby or whatever you go by these days. I know your Exa's child."

Peter's mouth was dry, but he managed to fumble out the words, "You do?"

"I've always known. It was a little too obvious what she was up to from the beginning. Why would she teach a child piano lessons?" He calmly took another sip from his drink while he stared at Peter.

"She didn't know then," Peter defended. "Neither one of us knew."

Ambrose chuckled a deep belly roll. "You believe that?"

"Yeah . . ." Peter's didn't think his gut could tightened any more but somehow he felt it wrench harder when he asked, "What do you believe?"

Ambrose swirled the liquid in his glass, then dumped it into his mouth. "Exa's a conniving, ruthless manipulator. She knew what she was doing. I believe she orchestrated it all from the beginning."

Peter felt the lines on his forehead wrinkle as these accusations weren't something he was expecting. "Orchestrated what?"

"Everything."

"How could she plan that? Peter asked in a defensive tone. "She thought I was dead."

"I think she gave birth to you and then gave you up for adoption with the understanding when you were older, she would be involved."

Peter let his lips bend down, disappointed in how this conversation was going. He didn't want to argue but he felt like he was being put on the spot and forced to defend Exa. "That's not how it happened at all."

Ambrose raised an eyebrow and smiled like he was amused. "And how would you know?"

"Because I know my parents and Exa have the same story. There's no way she could set that up."

"You believe what you want." He waved in a dismissing manner. "I see it a different way."

Perplexed at how Ambrose seemed to know so much about Peter, when he himself was only learning this stuff recently, he needed confirmation and felt himself fumble to ask, "So . . . this whole time when Exa was teaching me, you thought I-I was your son?"

"I don't have a son," Ambrose said flatly.

Peter swallowed hard. He hadn't expected to be welcomed with open arms, but Ambrose's abrasive frankness crushed his confidence. Then silence filled the dusty air. Ambrose poured himself another drink. It seemed to Peter there was nothing much else to say as Ambrose obviously wasn't going to welcome Peter. He inched toward the door, and said, "Well, I didn't mean to intrude. I wanted to say hi—"

"—You can leave or," Ambrose cut in.

Peter was hesitant to ask but he took the bait, "Or what?"

"Or. . ." Tilting his head a measure toward Peter, he said, "I will give you another chance to tell me why you're really here."

"I don't know what you mean."

Ambrose took a few measured steps closer to Peter. "Don't you want something from me?"

"How do you know? I mean, m-maybe," he stuttered, feeling the heat rise in his chest as this conversation wasn't going even close to how he thought it would.

He set his dark eyes in a lock on Peter. "I know your story. It's all over the Internet. I know you need a kidney."

Peter squeaked out, "I didn't realize you knew that much about me."

"Don't flatter yourself." He wagged a finger at Peter. "It's hard not to know your story with all the news coverage you get."

"I try not to pay attention to the media," Peter truthfully admitted.

"Are you surprised I know who you are?" Ambrose asked in a taunting manor.

He wasn't sure where he found his courage, but he managed to hold Ambrose's stare while he said, "Yeah. I guess, it makes me wonder if you knew all this, how come you never tried to talk to me?"

"Because I don't care." There was an echoing in his words, that stung right in the middle of Peter's heart but before Peter could ask another question, Ambrose took control of the conversation and said, "So, my turn to ask a question."

"W-What?"

"You want something from me . . . Something only I can give you."

Peter nodded like a shy schoolboy, completely blown away by the fact that Ambrose would know about his condition.

"What are you going to do for me?" Ambrose pried.

"W-What do you want?"

Ambrose paced in measured footsteps to the opposite side of the room and flexed his fingers together while he appeared to think. When he reached the other end of the room, but before he turned to look back, he said, "Record a song with me."

"What?" Peter thought he heard that wrong.

Turning back to face Peter, he trapped Peter's eyes and said, "Record a song with me while you're here."

"Why?" Peter could understand why an undiscovered artist would want a song recorded with him, because it would boost someone's career, but Ambrose's career was larger than his. There was no fame that he could lend to him, and their music styles weren't even on the same planet.

Ambrose smirked. "Maybe I'll tell you when we're done."

Peter raised a suspicious eyebrow toward him, and he felt a sinking feeling in his gut like he was trapped. On one hand it seemed like such an easy task, but he had enough sense to think there had to be a catch. To clarify, he asked, "You're saying all I need to do is record with you and then you will give me a kidney?"

"There's nothing else I want more, just as there is nothing else you want more."

"It's an offer I don't understand," Peter spoke slowly, "but I also can't refuse it." He hesitated, then asked, "When do you want to start?"

"Tomorrow will be good." Ambrose inclined his chin in acknowledgement of their deal and added, "Come with some inspiration."

"Okay," Peter said even more timidly.

"Oh, and . . ."

"Yeah."

"While we are working on the song . . ."

Peter squinted his eyes, feeling fooled because he had known there'd be a catch. "Yeah. What?"

"Stay here with me."

"Huh?" His voice raised in confusion. "What kind of deal is that?"

"It's the only deal you have on the table. Take it or leave it."

It seemed like such a ridiculous stipulation to put on a deal like that, Peter couldn't help but ask, "Why?"

"It's not so bad living in a castle." There was a rattle-snake gleam in

Ambrose's eye Peter didn't trust. He thought he could hear his mom telling him to run away and Exa's warning about staying away from Ambrose replayed in his ear as well.

"Ah, I . . . okay, I guess. I'll come over after I check out of my hotel in the morning."

"Splendid," Ambrose said, making the hairs on Peter's arm literally spike out. He had no idea what he was getting himself into but at this point he also had nothing to lose.

CHAPTER ELEVEN

"*H*ey Mom, I guess I'm gonna stay here," Peter said on the phone the next morning.

"You're not coming home?" Anne asked.

"Not for a while."

"Why?"

"It's France. I want to spend some time here."

"Did you see him?"

"I did. We hit it off right away." Peter cringed through the lie, and quickly added, "We even talked about writing some music together."

"Really?"

"Yeah, I know it seems a little weird, but I think he was excited to meet me. He's letting me stay at his place."

"Wow, that's sound so amazing that he is so open to receiving you. See, I knew it would all work out. I'm so happy for you," Anne gushed. Then her tone changed to one of concern and she asked, "Are you sure it's not too much for you to stay there, though.'"

"It's fine. Don't worry."

"What about your dialysis?"

"I already called a place here and I'm having my records sent. I should be able to get the same services here."

"So," Anne started in an inquiring tone, "does he know about the kidney?"

"Mom, you're asking too many questions."

"I don't mean to pry but I am just curious."

"We didn't really talk about it. I think we need to get to know each other first."

"I get this is a whole new world for you. And, I understand biology and how you would have a pull toward him, but I'm getting a 'be careful' vibe."

"What do you want me to do?" Peter asked, feeling exhausted, because he didn't see any other options. "Do you want to come here, stand over my shoulder, and make sure he's nice to me?"

"That's not a bad idea."

"*Mom.*"

"Okay, I know I need to let you live your life, but this is hard for me. How long are you staying?"

"A while."

"A month?"

"Longer than that."

"Okay then. If you're still there by the time the twins are in school, I'm going to come visit you," she stated firmly.

"You don't have to."

"I know, but I need to physically see you to know you are thriving. Deal?"

"Deal," Peter groaned. "Are you done chewing me out now?"

"Yes, but I have some news to tell you."

"What now?"

"I heard from Olivia."

"Oh."

"Gwen set the date for her wedding. It's right at the end of August.

Peter's voice got locked in the back of his throat.

"Are you there?"

"I'm here."

"Did you hear me? You're going to miss Gwen's wedding if you stay there too long."

"I would probably miss it anyway because I wasn't invited."

"You don't have to be invited. It's Gwen."

"Yeah, I know it's Gwen, but I was told to give her space."

"I don't think that means to miss her wedding."

"I do."

"Well, suit yourself."

"I will."

"Should I sign your name on a card?"

Peter thought for a moment, but having his mom sign his name on a card seemed like such a coward thing to do. "No, I can send one myself."

"Alright, well you call me every day or I'm hopping a flight to see you."

"Is that a threat?"

"It's a promise."

Peter ended the call, flung his duffle bag over his shoulder, and closed the hotel room door behind him. He had a cab waiting downstairs to take him to his new home. He didn't feel good about it, but he also didn't have another option.

CHAPTER TWELVE

*A*mbrose gave Peter keys to the house and a bedroom on the second floor, which was right up the grand staircase. Since the staircase was a huge challenge for Peter to climb with his limited mobility, he mostly stayed upstairs.

He had found his room in the same condition as the rest of the house, full of filth and in desperate need of cleaning which he quickly got right to. Then after he was exhausted from dusting, he dropped onto his bed, swiping through his emails on his phone—nothing from Gwen. A knock came from the door. Peter looked back to see Doc holding a tray of food.

"I noticed you have trouble with the staircase, so when you didn't come down for supper, I decided to bring you a sandwich and some pie." The corners of his lips curled up slightly and he added, "I love pie."

Peter's gaze softened. "Thank you."

Doc placed the tray on the dresser. "You know, I don't think Ambrose noticed your trouble with the stairs, but if you want I can say something to him and we can find a place for you to sleep downstairs."

"Nah, I don't want to be a bother. I'm not going to stay here long anyway."

"Very well then. I'm the butler, but until we get more staff, I'm sort of doing whatever, so if you need anything, let me know."

"Thank you." Peter watched Doc leave the room. Then he picked up one half of the sandwich. It looked like turkey. Feeling hungry and drained, he eagerly bit into it. He had spent two hours calling floral shops in Minnesota, trying to round up as many purple lilies as possible. *One thousand purple lilies should do the trick*. He wasn't going to be there to see Gwen get married, but he wanted her to know he cared. He had instructed the flower stores to line up vases all along the walls of the church so when Gwen walked down the aisle, his lilies would be there every step of the way. Just like he was giving her away because that's honestly how he felt . . .

∾

A week later, Peter joined Ambrose in his recording studio. He didn't forget what his mission was while he was here, and the faster he got this project done, the faster he could get home. Ambrose's recording studio wasn't as dusty as the rest of the house. Peter was at least able to breathe a little through his nose, so he relaxed on a rolling stool in the center of the room and asked, "So, what did you have in mind?"

"Our sounds are so different I think we could do like a crossroads thing and come up with something unique."

Peter sniffed, trying to clear his nose. "So, you want a song with lyrics?"

"We need lyrics or it's not a song." Ambrose picked up an acoustic guitar that was nearest him.

"I've never really written lyrics before."

"Now's a good time to start. What do you want to write about?"

With everything that Peter had been through these last few weeks, he was completely numb inside and his inner creativity had been drowned out. Not landing on any idea's worth speaking out, he shook his head. "I don't know."

"You got a girl?" Ambrose asked while he strummed lightly on his guitar strings, expertly adjusting the pitch to sound just right.

"No, just gave her away," he said a little too hopelessly.

Looking over his guitar at Peter, Ambrose smiled knowingly and said, "We can use that. Tell me something else about her."

"There's nothing to tell." He felt his spine stiffen, thinking about Gwen marrying Brad. "She's my friend and she's getting married."

"How does that make you feel?"

Peter sighed, annoyed. "Everyone keeps asking me that. Like I'm supposed to know what to do or how I should feel, but the only thing that keeps running through my head is I should've asked her first."

Ambrose pushed his lips out, while he mused, then pulled one corner of his mouth up and said, "Sounds like we just got our hook."

"Huh?"

"I like it. *I should've asked her first.*"

Peter rolled his eyes. "You've got to be kidding."

"That's what's bothering you. We need to write about it."

Crossing his arms loosely over his chest, he slumped down, and said, "It's not bothering me."

Ambrose smirked as he moved his fingers down the strings of the guitar, playing with a few chords.

"You're insane," Peter tried to talk him out of it, but it was no use and sure enough one week later, they had their song.

With a few days off before they were scheduled to meet with studio musicians to record, Peter was on his way out the door to dialysis when he realized he forgot his cell phone. He darted up the grand staircase. About halfway up, he stopped to rest. His legs were wobbly, and his balance was off as it seemed to have gotten so much worse since he arrived in France. His hip felt especially tight, causing his left foot to want to bend inward, even further than normal. Rubbing his hip joint, he then clenched his teeth, finished the climb, grabbed his phone, and returned to descend the stairs.

A couple steps down, his left foot bent inward when he stepped. When he placed his right foot next to it, he accidently stepped onto his protruding toe, lost his balance, and rolled headfirst, bellowing in pain all the way to the last step.

Doc was first to come running, and called for the ambulance. Ambrose soon followed. Miraculously, Peter was still fully conscious and able to converse. He grabbed a handful of tissues from Doc and wrapped them around his bleeding nose, squeezing it. It didn't feel broken.

"Can you move everything?" Ambrose asked.

"Yeah, I think so." Peter's voice was nasally as he pinched his nose shut. "I might be able to get up if you guys want to help me."

"No, I think if you would have seen the amount of summer saults you just did, you would want to get checked out first," Doc said.

"If you say so," Peter groaned and resigned to the fact that this was going to be a wasted day.

DOCTORS DETERMINED THAT NOTHING WAS BROKEN, BUT AFTER COMPARING Peter's past records to his current assessments, they referred him to a specialist who determined his muscle tone had weakened considerably thus affecting his balance. His doctors recommended physical therapy, which Peter was no stranger too, but the next word they said was a life changer—wheelchair.

Peter convinced himself the chair would be temporary, and he still had his cane for when he felt strong enough to walk. The regression diagnosis only solidified Peter's desire to get his recording project done so he would move past this season in his life and get home where he knew he would feel stronger.

While Peter was getting fitted for his new wheels, Doc took it upon himself to move Peter's stuff down to the main level. There were no bedrooms down there, so he made up the couch in the parlor for him. Then he grabbed a dust rag and started to wipe the furniture down and that's where Peter found him when he wheeled his chair into the room. "You don't have to clean everything. I'll be fine."

Kneeling on his hands and knees, his belly barely missed grazing the floor while Doc crawled around, wiping the table legs. "I don't mind. This place could use a good cleaning." Then he sat back on his heels, looking at Peter. "Did your friend get ahold of you?"

"What friend?"

"She called the house phone this morning when you were gone. She said she was flying into town and was hoping to stay here for a few days. I sent Leo to grab her from the airport."

"Was it my mom?" Peter grabbed his cell and looked through his calls for a missed call. "Did she say her name?"

"Yeah, it was Quin or something."

"Gwen?" Peter sat up straighter in his wheelchair. "What did she say?"

"Just that she would be arriving this evening. Leo should be back soon."

Peter was mentally and physically exhausted from therapy, but the thought of seeing Gwen boosted his energy as well as thoroughly confused him.

"Would you like me to serve you tea when she arrives, or perhaps a late dinner?" Doc asked.

Peter scratched the back of his head, wondering why Gwen never called his phone. "Tea would be fine."

CHAPTER THIRTEEN

Still learning to use the electric controls on his wheelchair, Peter drove himself to the library where Gwen was waiting for him. He watched how Gwen's eyes went from sparkling with excitement to quickly switching to display worry when she saw Peter's chair. She stepped forward, and hugged him. "What happened?"

"Nothing really. It's temporary until I can get through physical therapy."

"I'm sorry." Her lips bent down even more. "I didn't know."

"It's really no big deal and not worth talking about." He steered himself next to the tea cart and took the cup of Earl Grey tea Doc was offering him. "Did you meet Doc?"

"I did."

"He offered to have dinner for you, but I said tea would be fine. Unless, are you hungry?"

"Nah, I've been munching all day. But thank you." Gwen sat back down on the couch. Doc handed Gwen her cup of perfectly steeped tea. Smiling a little coyly, she placed the saucer on her lap, and looked back at Doc, and said, "Thank you."

"So . . . I didn't know you were coming," Peter said.

"Yeah, it's a surprise. I hope that's okay."

"It's a great surprise. How long are you staying?"

"Couple days."

"May I get you anything else?" Doc asked.

"No, thank you," Peter said, and they both watch Doc quietly leave the room.

Once he was out of hearing range, Gwen giggled as she blew on the liquid at the edge of her teacup. "You have servants now? And tea time."

Peter smiled broadly from the sound of her giggle. "I guess so. Did he get you set up in a room?"

"Yeah, he did. It's upstairs. This house is amazing. I can't wait to get the whole tour."

"Doc could give you one." He took a sip of tea and then set his cup down. After Gwen didn't reply, Peter searched his brain for a new topic to talk about. He didn't understand why, but he oddly for the first time ever felt nervous around her. "So, how's your mom?"

"She's good. She got her hours cut at the post office, but it's been okay." Then sitting back up straighter, she inclined her chin, and said, "Actually, I talked to your mom the other day to find out where you were staying. She told me you weren't coming to the wedding."

"About that—" Peter ran a hand through the back of his hair. "I know it would be a long flight, and I'm in the middle of a project."

Her eyes were wide and unwavering while she steadied them on Peter's and asked, "Is that all?"

Peter held her gaze, feeling like there was something Gwen wasn't saying. "What do you mean?"

She lowered her eyes all the way to her cup, and let her fingers play with the edge of the saucer. Then in a soft voice she said, "I was worried that maybe you were mad at me."

"You haven't talked to me in weeks, and you think *I'm* the mad one?"

"Aside from that." She let her eyes meet his again, but this time there was a sadness in them when she asked, "Are we okay?"

Now it was Peter's turn to look down at his cup like they were playing some weird game. "Aside from you trying to cut me out. I guess so."

"Good, because I could never get married if we weren't good." Gwen smiled timidly, but her voice was still unconvinced.

Taking a breath to clear this conversation, Peter leaned back in his chair, looking at her. Her boney knees stuck out from under her yellow floral skirt. She looked a little skinnier than normal, but she was always on the thin side, as she struggled to keep weight on. She looked the same as she always did, but then there was something different about her too.

"What?" Gwen asked from behind her teacup.

"I didn't say anything."

"You're staring at me."

He blinked his eyes and looked toward the window, and then back at her. "It's just, you look pretty."

Gwen laughed self-consciously. "Oh, well, thank you. I feel a little jet-lagged."

"It is a long flight, but you should be able to rest up. How long before you have to go back?"

"You already asked me that. Do you not want me here?"

"Yes, I want you here. I was just asking. I guess, I'm surprised you're here." Peter's words started to come out in a ramble like once he got started talking, he didn't really know where to stop and he went on. "And all the sudden. I'm curious because for weeks you don't return any of my calls or texts. Your mom tells me to butt out of your life forever, and now I've left the country, and you show up. I'm wondering what happened."

"I'm sorry." Her lips straightened when she said, "I didn't mean to intrude—"

"—You're not intruding," Peter interrupted, "but what the heck is up?"

"I'm sorry . . . that I didn't respond to your texts." She looked down at her cup briefly, before raising her chin again. "I've been busy planning the wedding."

"That's bull." Peter let out a sarcastic laugh. "I was told Brad wouldn't let you talk to me. You were avoiding me. Don't lie and tell me you were busy."

Gwen released a sigh that held a tone of hurt. "I'm sorry. It's just. I'm sorry. That's it. Can we not talk about what a jerk I've been?" Her soulful blue eyes pleaded. "I'm here to visit you now and it's only for a few days, so can you forgive me?"

He wanted to ask her so much more, but he bit down on his lip and then relented. "Okay, sure."

"Good."

"So, what do you want to do while you are here?"

Gwen's face broke out into a huge smile as she blurted out, "I want to go to Paris!"

"Why?" He asked flatly, as the thought of leaving the house with his new wheels seemed daunting.

"It's Paris! Who doesn't want to go to Paris? I looked online, and they have day trips from here where you can take a bus. It's super cheap."

Peter was quiet for the moment, as he pondered the irony of taking Gwen to Paris—the city of love—and one of the most romantic places on earth while she was engaged to Brad. Nothing made sense to him anymore, but after a while he said, "We don't have to take a bus. Leo can drive us."

Gwen's grin got even wider. "You and all your servants."

Peter laughed. Feeling good to laugh with her, he knew he missed her easy-going nature despite how complicated their relationship was getting.

"What?" She asked, while she gave him an inquiring eye.

"What do you mean what? I didn't say anything."

"You keep looking at me all weird."

Peter looked down, suddenly feeling bashful on top of his mounting confusion. *There's something different about you and nothing makes sense anymore.* He wanted to make her happy though, so without hesitating, he said, "We could go tomorrow?"

Her shoulders pulled into an excited cringe, and she squealed out, "I was hoping you'd say that!"

"I'll let Leo know tonight."

"That would be awesome. I can't wait." Gwen beamed at him, and then said, "I'm never going to be able to sleep tonight because it's just too exciting."

"I can't believe you aren't worn out from your flight."

"It wasn't too bad. I thought it would be scarier to fly over the ocean, but it wasn't. I even had a window seat."

"I don't get scared flying." Peter picked up on the new topic, and continued, "Maybe when I was little, but since I have flown so much it doesn't bother me."

"I don't get scared normally, but that's a lot of water. I kept thinking about having to make a water landing."

"Why would you even think about that? You're gonna have nightmares about swimming with the sharks."

"Yeah, I was already picturing myself learning how to communicate and make friends with the frogs."

"Frogs don't live in the ocean."

"They don't?" Her nose scrunched. "Because they don't have lily pads?"

"No, because they would die. They are freshwater fish. Didn't you learn that in school?"

"Nah, I probably missed that day for chemo," Gwen replied in a dismissing way."

"Well . . ." Peter looked out the window, and the natural sunlight was already gone. "It's probably too late to go anywhere tonight, but would you want to watch a movie or something?"

"Only if I can pick."

"Okay, but I call no Elvis movies."

"You can't call that."

"Yeah, I can."

Gwen pushed her lips out. "Fine, I pick *The Wizard of Oz*."

"That's not much better," Peter teased but willingly moved his chair forward. "We can go stream it back in my room."

"Okay." Gwen followed him into his room, and she sat next to Peter on his couch, sharing the same blanket— Gwen's pink Elvis blanket she insisted she couldn't watch a movie without. Peter turned the movie on with the remote and then slouched onto the armrest, pushing his feet into the middle cushion of the couch so his toes touched Gwen's. Gwen joined Dorothy in saying her lines to the movie out loud.

"If you're gonna do that the whole movie, I'm shutting it off now," Peter grumbled.

"You're a fun hater." Gwen glared at him, pulling the blanket up further.

"No I'm not. It's distracting."

"From what?" She held her hand out in a questioning manner. "We've watched this movie some zillion times. You know what's going on. Don't you remember you used to act it out with me?"

"That's sort of one of those things I want to forget," Peter said while maintaining his gaze on the T.V.

"Why? You made an awesome Lion."

"I hated being the Lion. That's the worst one to be." He shot a quick glance at her and asked, "Who wants to be a coward? Paul and Tane always forced me to do the dumbest stuff. Stupid brothers."

"You're lucky you have them. I have no siblings. It's so boring. I always envied your big family. That's why I loved it at your house."

"It wasn't ever boring there, that's for sure." Peter reached under the blanket and squeezed her toes. "You always made an awesome Dorothy though."

"Thanks." She looked down as her cheeks pinked. "I practiced a lot. I always wanted one of those bikes from the movie."

With his brows bending down, he stated, "You had a bike."

"Yeah, I had one, but I thought that one was way better."

"At least you got to ride a bike," he said sarcastically as his eyes flew back to the screen.

She looked thoughtfully at him. "You never rode one?"

"Nah."

"Not even one with training wheels?"

"One time I did," his voice was quiet, hinting of something bad.

"What happened?"

"I was riding, trying to keep up with Tane and Paul. They told me to go home because I was slowing them down. So, I left my bike, thinking I would be faster on two feet. They sped away as fast as they could, telling me to run. They laughed so hard as I struggled to keep up, and I ended up collapsing on the trail and couldn't move. My legs had quit. My dad came to rescue me after I didn't show up for dinner and Tane confessed. It was humiliating. After that, I had an aversion to riding bike." Looking down, now rubbing his joints, he said in an even softer voice. "It was for the *cool* kids."

"That's terrible. I can't believe your mom didn't make them be nice to you."

"She tried, but she didn't see everything. That's brothers. You're not missing anything."

Gwen grabbed the remote that was sitting next to Peter and turned the volume down. He looked back at her with furrowed eyebrows.

"I was wondering . . ." Her eyes lightened bringing in a new layer of sensitivity.

"Now what?" Feeling his throat tighten, not ready to hear anything else that would confuse him, he did his best to remain calm.

"I'm serious now. I want to know how you dealt with it when you were little. What did you do when you realized you were *different*—like you wouldn't be able to ride bike like the other kids."

Peter rubbed the edge of the fleece blanket as he studied his memories. "I don't think I ever had a moment like that. I think it's always been my reality."

"Hmmm," Gwen said softly.

"Why?"

"Just wondering." She stared off into the room, not focusing on any one thing. Then she added, "I think I've had a few moments like that recently—where I've realized my life is going to be less than other people's."

"Less?" He asked, now concerned about her tone. "It's not less. Just different."

"It feels like less to me."

"How can it be less?" He leaned forward, trying to get a better look at her now somber expression. Feeling like he needed to cheer her up, he forced himself to bring up the one thing he didn't want to talk about, and he even put a fake smile on his face when he said, "You're getting married. That's amazing."

"I am lucky there." Her frown melted, and her lips curled up into a wistful smile. "I'm blessed to have met Brad. I can't imagine my life without him. Some people live a long life without love, and I might have a shorter one, but at least I have love."

Peter swore he tasted vomit in his mouth, and he fought every urge he had to not gag. Lucky for him, Gwen changed the subject, by reaching back under the blanket, and placing a hand on his foot "Pete," she said to get his attention while she squeezed his toes.

"Yeah."

"You made a great Lion, but you were never a coward. You've always been the bravest person I know," she added in a quiet voice.

Peter's heart started to race.

She continued, "I don't know what I would have done if I were in your shoes. You'll always be my biggest hero."

After a moment of not knowing what to say, Peter grinned and said, "I'm glad you're here. I missed you."

"I missed you too."

Then they settled into watching the movie, until it was late into the night, and they were both dosing off. "Boy, I can't keep my eyes open." Gwen covered her mouth as her lips opened into a huge yawn. "Do you mind if I go to bed?"

"Go ahead," Peter said, barely opening his eyes, from where he had passed out on the couch. "I'm exhausted too."

She carefully stood to not wake him more and headed to the door, paused, and leaned against the frame, turning back to look at him, resting peacefully on his couch. "Night, Pete. See you in the morning."

"Night," he replied sleepily.

She giggled. "Tomorrow we go to *Pari*."

Pulling one eye opened all the way, he glanced at her all giddy in the door and said, "You're such a nerd."

"I love being a nerd." She winked and whispered, "Love ya. Night." Then quietly disappeared from the doorway, leaving Peter now fully awake with a new realization—*That's it. The look she has. I know what's different about her now. She's in love, but it ain't me. I don't know why I didn't believe it before, but she honestly thinks she's in love with Brad.* He listened to her footsteps patter down the hall. "Love you too," he whispered.

CHAPTER FOURTEEN

*P*eter watched Gwen bounce down the grand staircase, wearing a yellow, suede backpack with a giant Elvis Presley button pinned to it. "I can't believe we are going to Paris!" she squealed.

"I thought you came to France to see me."

"I did. But it's super awesomeness you are so close to Paris."

"So it's a convenience thing, then?"

Totally, and I spent all my tips I saved from the coffee shop to fly over here, so I went online last night and printed off a list of stuff we can do for free." She handed him the list.

Taking the list, he immediately folded it in half without looking at it and pushed it back at her. "We can do whatever you want. It's okay if it costs money. I can pay."

"I don't want you to think I'm using you for a free trip to Paris."

Peter smirked. "It's starting to look that way, but it's okay if you are. I'm just glad I finally get to see you."

Doc came around the corner from the kitchen, holding a basket covered with a white linen cloth. "I packed you some goodies for the trip." He handed the basket to Leo, who had appeared in the doorway, ready to load up the car.

"Ah, that's so sweet," Gwen said. "You didn't have to."

"It's no problem. Just some pastries I picked up this morning on my walk." Doc winked at her and rubbed his swollen belly. "I've already had several. You'll enjoy them."

Gwen giggled, letting her eyes rest fondly back on Doc. "I'm sure we will. Thanks."

Lifting his arm, motioning to the door, Peter asked, "Shall we head out?"

"We shall." Gwen agreed, as she moved forward, joining Peter right by his side.

Once in the car, Peter watched the landscape out his window, wondering so many things. He was confused about Gwen being here when she had worked so hard to shut him out, but he was also still nervous about his project with Ambrose and how it was still sitting unfinished. Gwen broke his thoughts, by saying, "I can't believe you just ran away to France. It's so beautiful here."

"I didn't run away. I came here to find Ambrose."

"Is he even here? I didn't see him."

"He was. Doc said this morning he left last night for a short trip. We recorded a song." Peter's voice trailed off and he felt his cheeks warm when he remembered he wrote the song for Gwen.

"How was that?" She asked with enthusiasm in her voice.

"Fine."

"His music is so much louder than yours."

"His music is all tempo. But, at least with my piano solos he has some melody. It makes it tolerable."

"I can't wait to hear it."

"It's uh, not finished yet," Peter lied because he didn't want to have to tell her how much he was thinking about her.

"Your mom said you sung on it?"

"A little. Ambrose did most of the vocals."

"I bet you sound awesome."

"Or something else like that."

"I totally picture it being like a smoky, soulful growl."

"It's called singing. Not growling and I would say that's not even close. Maybe more like Micky Mouse." Peter picked up his phone and scrolled through a screen and then held it up for her to see. "I got a list of museums. I'm sure you've heard of the Louvre. Or not . . ." he added when she didn't respond.

Her eyes were fixed on something outside the window—a row of birds was lined up parallel with the car and flew in union with them. "How do they know where to go?" She wondered out loud, rolled her window down, sticking her arm out, extending it toward them like she wanted to fly away too.

"I think it's instinct."

"But they just follow the first one and they know automatically they can trust that bird is going to know where to go?"

"I don't know if they think about it so much. They're just birds. I think they just fly around all day."

Her face was serious, and at times pained as she watched the birds. "But, do you ever think one bird might be scared to follow the other birds? Like maybe she has her own ideas about what she should do? But she follows because that's what she has to do."

Peter knew she wasn't talking about birds anymore. "Maybe she follows them because she's scared to be alone?"

Gwen blinked her eyes like she just realized she wasn't talking to herself. "Oh, yeah, I don't know; it's crazy how nature works." She rolled the window up and sat back in her seat. "Uh, the Louvre, huh? That's sounds so, I don't know. Now that I think of it, it would be great if we had more time, but I don't feel like waiting in lines all day and being in a huge crowd. I would rather go stroll through a beautiful park and people watch."

"What about the Eiffel Tower?"

Gwen wrinkled her nose. "Too cliché."

Peter smiled to himself. That's why he liked Gwen. She was laid back and easy to please. "Okay, I'll tell Leo to find us a park that's not *cliché.*"

LEO LET THEM OUT OF THE CAR AT PARC MONCEAU—A BEAUTIFUL SHADED park with trails, statues, and an 1800th century colonnade.

"This is perfect." Gwen grabbed her bag and Doc's basket out of the car, surveying her surroundings. Leo helped Peter into his chair and offered to push him, but Peter declined in French.

"When did you learn French?" Gwen asked, as she fell into step next to Peter as they both headed down the path.

"Still learning. I have an app on my phone where I learn a few words a day."

"That's awesome. I want to learn too."

"Download the app. It's super easy." Peter lifted his chin, motioned forward and said, "Hey, I gotta check out that bridge."

"Let's walk over there and set up our stuff to relax."

Peter wheeled his chair next to a bench that Gwen had picked out. She put her sunglasses over her eyes to shield the noon sun.

"Shall we see what surprise is in our basket?" Gwen asked, as she was already pulling the towel up at the corner.

Peter rubbed his hands together to stir up the anticipation. "Oh man, it's like Christmas."

She unwrapped the first package, uncovering the mystery pastry. "They look all wrinkled."

"Those are angel wings. I saw those before." Peter pulled one out and broke it in half, handing part of it to her.

Taking it from him, she bit into it, and nodded her head, letting her eyes close while she savored the texture. "Yep, these are delicious."

Peter wasn't interested in eating, as his stomach had been a wreck since Gwen had arrived. He surveyed the park, taking in all the lush greenery. "I could eat duck doo in this park and it would taste great."

Gwen let out a giggle. "Gross. Thanks for the visual."

"Just saying."

"Whatever." Gwen chewed slowly, then asked, "So, you wanna tell me about the chair?"

Peter's mouth got instantly dry. "That's a little terse."

"Sorry, I didn't mean it to be." She kept her head tucked and picked at her angel wing. "I guess, whatever. You don't have to talk about it."

"It is what it is." He shrugged, easily letting go of the topic, but he also had a question that was bothering him. "Since we are being so open in our questions, you want to tell me about the wedding?"

"Sure, it's going to be at the church I was baptized in, and Brad's sister is going to be my maid of honor. We picked out a yellow dress for her, and daisies are going to be my flower. I wanted lilies, you know . . ." She hesitated and motioned to him. "They have so much meaning to me, but Brad said he doesn't like lilies, so we went with daisies, and my mom is—"

Peter interrupted, "I don't want to hear about dresses, and flowers."

Her lips turned down, while the rest of her face froze. "I thought you said you wanted to talk about my wedding."

Peter rubbed his forehead, trying to find the words. When nothing sophisticated came to him, he flicked his hand out toward her and asked, "Why?"

"Why what?"

Leaning forward, making sure he could grab her eye contact he asked, "Why are you marrying him?"

"That's kind of rude." She visually stiffened, sitting up straighter. "You know, he said you were negative about him, and I didn't believe it, but now I'm starting to see it. What do you have against him?"

"How about what don't I have against him?"

"He has done nothing to you."

Peter dropped his jaw wide open.

Gwen continued to hold her eyes in communion with his, but her eyes were quickly clouding with a protectiveness. "What is that face for?"

Peter shook his head, feeling like there was no use to this conversation. "Tell me, what did Brad do to you?"

All of his concerns about Brad, started to bubble in his gut, and he weighed whether or not he should say something. He knew Gwen honestly cared for Brad, but there were so many warning signs. As hard as he tried, he couldn't sit back and let her stay blind to them all. Giving into his own gut, he said, "I don't want to have to be the one to point this out, but last night I saw something in you. I saw you really do think you love him, and I can't sit back when I know he's not the one for you. I know you want him to be the one, but I have to be honest, he's using you."

"No he's not." Her eyes narrowed, then flinched. "He loves me."

Wanting to break the news gently but also not wanting to sugar coat anything, he reached out and placed his hand on her knee and gently said, "I saw your insurance papers and how he's the *only* beneficiary for a two-million-dollar policy. Don't you think it's a little convenient he gets money when you die? Oh yeah, and let's not forget you refused cancer treatment, so you are, in fact, dying."

"You looked at my stuff!" She pulled away, brushing his hand off her knee. "You're insane. That's not how it is at all. I trust he'll do the right thing with the money, because we *trust* each other."

"Really? Think about it. You have cancer. What nineteen-year-old guy would rush into marrying someone who is dying? Was it his idea for you to refuse treatment?"

"No! And is it really impossible for you to think someone could actually love me enough to want to marry me?"

"No, that's not impossible at all . . . " Peter's voice trailed off as he looked past her into the distance. "You obviously don't see things the way I do, or did."

"What am I supposed to see?"

"I'm done talking."

"Don't shut me out."

"Naw, you already did that first." Peter pushed his chair away from the bench, wheeling it toward the bridge.

"Where are you going?" Gwen followed him.

"Gonna feed the ducks."

"Now?"

"I can't talk anymore. I'm going to end up saying something I might regret." Peter stopped on top of the bridge and inched toward the ledge. He had half an angel wing which he had been gripping tightly in his hand. It was mushy, and he peeled off the edge a little at a time, forcefully chucking it into the water. Three ducks raced trying to get the pastry, squawking defensively the whole time. *It would be so much easier if the only thing I wanted in life was some pastry crumbs like these dumb ducks.*

CHAPTER FIFTEEN

"I seriously can't believe you made me watch *Barefoot in the Park*, again," Peter groaned as he awoke the next day. He had crashed on his couch, and Gwen had fallen asleep on the floor next to him. They had stayed up late into the morning hours, too excited to sleep after their trip.

She rolled over to face him and asked in a dreamy voice, "How is it not your favorite movie?"

"It's so cheesy."

"It's *so* beautiful."

"You always had an over-simplistic view of relationships. If all I had to do was walk barefoot in the park to find love, then I'd probably never put on shoes, but it's not that simple." Gwen never responded, so Peter lifted his chin to look over the edge of the couch at her. She was rapidly texting on her phone. He waited for her to get done, but she just kept texting, and then got up and said, "I need to call Brad." Not waiting for a reply, she darted from the room.

Peter was dipping his French bread into hot chocolate in the kitchen when Gwen found him later. She kept her head down, as she pulled up a stool next to him. He pushed the plate of bread in front of her and motioned to the hot water in the tea kettle. She took some bread and pulled off a piece, stuffing it into her mouth, and sullenly chewed it. After she finished it, she sighed heavily. "I have to go home today. Brad booked me a flight. Leo's going to take me to the airport in an hour."

"Is everything okay?"

Gwen rested her elbows on the table and sunk her chin into her palms. "Brad's worried about me being over here. He got a little freaked out."

Peter continued chewing his bread without speaking.

"I mean, it was sort of a surprise to him that I was over here."

"You didn't tell him you were coming?"

"Nah, he doesn't really understand about us."

"So, does that have something to do with why you called the house phone and not me?"

"You might not have noticed," she gave him a sideways glance, "but I think he's jealous of you. He gets super sensitive about things when I bring you up."

"I had no clue," Peter said, letting heavy sarcasm ring in his voice.

Gwen let out another huge sigh. "I wish he would understand I need you in my life. You're my best friend."

Peter knew better than to say anything to make her feel bad about having to leave but he wasn't really ready to say goodbye yet. "Can I ride with you to the airport, or will *Brad* get mad?"

Gwen glared. "I wish you could see him the way I do. He's not a bad guy. He gets self-conscious around you because he knows how much you mean to me, and he wants you to like him."

Peter pushed his chair away from the table. "I'm so over talking about Brad. If this is the last morning I have with you, can we talk about something else?"

"Fine. What do you want to do? Oh, I still haven't seen the gardens yet." She motioned out the window. "Will you show me?"

"Anything but sitting here and talking about that person I don't want to talk about."

Later, Peter wheeled his chair into the airport to wait in line with Gwen. The chaos around them from hundreds of people was muted by the heaviness in his heart. "Ugh, it looks like my flight's delayed an hour," Gwen read a text alert on her phone. "I don't want to go through security yet, if I can stay out here with you. Wanna sit over there?" She pointed to an empty corner. Peter nodded, and wheeled over to the corner.

Gwen pulled up a chair, sitting next to him. She put her phone away. "Well, thanks for putting up with me. It was great to see you." Her eyes were sincere.

"You're welcome." Peter forced a smile, even though he felt nothing but dread.

"What are you thinking about?"

Peter had a feeling of doom in his chest. He knew Gwen was getting on that plane and was going to go home to be with Brad—*forever*. He was okay with that, mostly. "Truth?" Peter asked.

"Yeah, I want the truth."

"It's really not any of my business. I want you to be happy, but I have to ask, if the guy you claim to be in love with doesn't want you to hang out with your best friend, do you really think he's the one?"

Gwen's lips tightened. "Do you really want to fight with me about Brad, again?"

"I'm not trying to fight. This isn't really about Brad either. It's more about you and I. I don't understand why Brad gives you the ultimatum that I can't be in your life, and you listen to him."

"It's because I know he doesn't understand our friendship and it stresses him out, and I love him. I don't want to stress him out, so I feel like I should honor that request."

Peter scowled at her.

"It's hard to explain, but when you're in love you do things to make the other person happy. Just wait. You'll see someday when it happens to you," Gwen added. "I wish you could be happy for me."

Peter continued to glare at her.

"What?"

"I'm not going to lie. I don't think Brad's the one. I think you are rushing into this because you're scared this is your only chance."

"Really? How would you know?"

"Because I know you."

"Well, then who do you think is the one?"

"Are you really asking me that?"

"Yeah, tell me if you know."

Peter bit his lip and then before he lost his courage he blurted out, "Let me ask you this . . . What can he give you that I can't?"

Gwen's face froze.

Peter continued, "I never saw it before, but this summer made me realize you're *my Gwen*. You've always been my Gwen. Help me understand why him?"

Gwen frantically shook her head like she was unwilling to listen to his words, but Peter continued, knowing this was the last chance he'd had to say these things to her. "You gotta be honest with me because I need to know how something I feel is so perfect, doesn't feel like that to you."

"I don't want to lie to you, but I can't tell you the truth."

Peter jerked his head back in annoyance. "What do you mean you can't tell me the truth? So there is a reason?"

"Pete, please." She lowered her voice, looking around behind her to make sure no one could hear then. Then she said, "I'm leaving in a few minutes. Let's not have this conversation now. I love you. You know that."

"Yeah, but you have a reason to why you could never be *in love* with me. Tell me."

She turned from him and gathered her bags. "I should get in line."

"No." He put his arms out to stop her. "You aren't going anywhere until you tell me why. Why Brad? I need to know. You owe it to me to tell me why."

"Can I have a hug?" She leaned in, completely ignoring his pleas. "I'm leaving now."

As she leaned in, he pulled her in closer and wrapped his other arm around her. He moved his head next to her ear, and whispered, "It kills me to see you with him." Gwen pulled away; tears glistened in her eyes. He continued, sounding angry, "I have a hard time thinking you fled all the way to France to see me right before you get married, if it wasn't for a reason. You're going back to your fiancé today, but you should see the look of doom on your face. It's all over your face you'd rather stay here. Can you be honest with me?" He leaned closer and whispered in her ear again. "Can you tell me you don't love me, and I will leave you alone?"

Gwen sniffed. "No, I can't say that, because I think I do love you."

His eyes got watery. "If you love me, then tell me why you won't let yourself give us a chance. You don't have to leave. Stay here with me. Forever is a long time to spend if you chose the wrong guy."

"Not for me," Gwen's voice cracked.

Peter grabbed both of her hands and squeezed. "It doesn't matter if it's only a day. I know you have this messed up thought you aren't getting what you deserve out of life, but to me it seems like you are giving up. What is this reason you can't just stay with me? Can it really be so bad you would refuse to be with me?"

"I can't say." She folded her bottom lip in, looking at him, her eyes filled with fear.

He glared at her. Now he was furious. *I was honest with you. You can't even tell me the truth. Brad's a loser. He doesn't even have a job. All he cares about his flexing his biceps in the mirror. Oh yeah, he's so tough. That's the only thing he has that I don't. So what. . . is that what you want? Some meat head guy who can walk around all . . . walk around. Who can walk around, walk around, walk around.* The words rang in his head like a gonging of a bell, over and over, making him lightheaded.

"Are you okay?" Gwen leaned forward, touching his arm. "You look like you're gonna pass out."

Peter locked his eyes on hers. "It's my chair, isn't it?"

"Huh?"

"You won't be with me because of my disability."

Her eyes popped open wide.

"Don't lie to me. Say it. Tell me the reason you don't want to be with me is because of my disability."

"No."

"Then say it isn't true."

She shut her eyes, and tears fell down her cheeks. She wiped them off with the back of her hand. An announcement came over the intercom announcing pre-boarding for her flight. "I gotta go." She looked to the security line. "I'm gonna miss my flight."

Peter was numb and in total disbelief that she could even consider leaving in this moment. She grabbed his hand, looked at him, and said, "It's just too hard, Pete."

"I disagree," he said stubbornly.

Gwen's eyes softened and she leaned her head forward, letting it rest against his forehead for a moment before she lifted it back up and said slowly, "Pete, I know you know, but cancer's prolly going to win this time—"

"—Gwen," Peter interrupted as he squeezed her hand again.

"No, it's okay." She shook her head, in a reassuring way, placing a hand on his chest to stop him from talking. "Let me say this. You will hate me for saying it, but I will hate myself more if I let you think there's something wrong with you."

"Why you can't be with a cripple?"

Gwen grimaced. "Stop it. I don't see you like that. You're amazing, and you're right. We do fit together perfectly." She looked away. "So I accept my life is gonna be less."

"Stop saying it's less."

"Let me finish. I don't think I could do that to you." Gwen wiped another tear, and in a tiny voice she squeaked out, "I mean, I'm just going to die." Her words got muffled and Peter could barely hear them as she continued, "I'm sorry. This makes me the biggest jerk, but you wanted the truth. So, there it is." As soon as Gwen got the words out, the pre-boarding announcement came on again, and she looked to the line. "Pete, I gotta go. But this kills me. What are you thinking?"

"I didn't know you could be so callous."

Gwen met his eyes, and said, "Cancer does that."

He glared at her.

"Please, forget about me," she whispered before pulling away and leaving.

CHAPTER SIXTEEN

A week later, Peter met his mom at the airport. Her mouth dropped opened when she saw him. "What happened?"

"Nothing. I'm just having issues with my balance and feel more comfortable in the chair."

"Oh wow, you should've said something." She examined Peter for a fast moment before changing her expression back to her concerned mom face. "Did you see a doctor? What about therapy?"

"I'm doing therapy. I'm fine. It's an issue with my muscle tone being low." He pushed his chair forward, ready for a new topic. "Let's get your bag. I think we go this way."

Anne followed him down the corridor to the baggage claim. "I have dreamed of coming to France my whole life. What have you seen?"

Peter made a left turn and said, "I've seen the thrilling inside of the therapy place and the dazzling dialysis center. Oh, and Gwen and I went to a park in Paris."

"How was Gwen's visit?"

"Fine."

"Fine as in it went well, or fine as in you don't want to talk about it?"

"Too many questions, Mom."

"Okay, I'll mind my own business."

"Here we go." He stopped and tilted his head toward a small hoard of people. There's the luggage."

Anne walked up to the conveyor belt that was spitting out bags. They watched as bags circulated around, waiting for her bag. "It's blue," Anne said. "I didn't want to check a black bag because I know everyone has a black bag."

"Is that it?" Peter pointed to a mid-sized rolling bag.

"Yep." She pushed her way through the people and grabbed her bag, pulling the handle out to roll it behind her. "Okay. Now what?"

"I have a car waiting outside. We can go to the house and get you settled. If you want to go out for dinner later, we can. I don't have anything going on the rest of the day."

"Sure." Anne walked, and Peter rolled next to her. His breath was heavy sounding, causing Anne to become concerned and she asked, "Do you always have to push that thing around?"

"This is just the travel chair. It folds nicely. I have a motorized one at the house. The doctors were worried about my hands not being able to push this one, but I didn't want to get fat and lazy, so we compromised."

"Does it bother your fingers?"

"I've haven't noticed anything worse than normal, but I'm usually not going far distances."

"Well, it's nice to have an option."

They left through the exit door and stood on the street where a row of cabs and rental vehicles waited. Leo waved at Peter.

"That's Leo. He's Ambrose's personal driver." They stopped on the curb and Leo walked over, taking Anne's bag before helping her into the back seat.

"Bonjour," Leo said.

Anne's mouth turned into a wide grin as she got excited about getting to practice French. "Bonjour."

"Leo doesn't speak English, so he's not being rude by not talking to us. He just doesn't understand it," Peter said. Leo helped Peter out of his chair, assisting him into the front seat before folding the chair and placing it into the trunk. Peter turned slightly to look back at his mom. "I'd sit by you, but there is more leg room in the front and I find I get crampier when I sit in back."

"That's fine," Anne said, climbing into her own spot in the back sit. Then Leo slid into the driver's seat and drove out.

"How's everyone else?" Peter started a new conversation.

"Good," Anne spoke loudly, projecting her voice to the front seat. "Paul said the coffee shop turned a nice profit for this quarter. He found an assistant manager to help him because his school schedule is about to get crazy. And your music school is still sitting there. We boarded up some of the windows, and I guess it will be waiting for you when you get back. It needs more personal direction."

"I don't know when that will be."

"It's fine. It's been there forever. It's not going to hurt anything. Oh, and Marie got back from Uganda. I think she's glad to be back, but you know how she is. She's already planning the next mission. She's trying to talk your dad into doing a longer one with her next time. She has been helping at the coffee shop, too. She loves the tips."

Peter smiled, picturing his medical, nerd sister waiting tables. "She probably has to do all she can not to take people's blood pressures when she sees them get a caffeine buzz," he joked.

"She likes it. Oh, what else? Well, the twins have school, so they are busy. Oh, and guess what Shiloh is doing?"

"What?"

"He's restoring that Chevy in the garage, and he *loves* it."

"Really? I can see him being a car guy."

"It fits him." Anne smiled when she saw Peter's reflection in the window. "Boy, it feels like you have been gone a lot longer."

Peter was silent.

Leo slowed down to pull into the driveway. While he punched in the code on the gate, Anne marveled, "Wow, is this the house?"

"Yep."

"I can't wait to see it."

"It will be interesting." Peter tried not to hold his breath. It was a coping mechanism he started after Gwen left, but it seemed like each day that passed he was having to use the practice even more than the previous day.

Doc greeted them both, helping Anne take her bag up the stairs to the room which Peter had previously occupied. No one informed her it had been Peter's and she was still clueless to the accident, and everyone preferred it to stay that way.

Doc had invited them for tea in the library. "Ambrose has meetings this week, but he'll be back to meet you before you leave," Peter explained.

"I can't wait to meet him."

Doc carried a tray into the room and set it on the desk. "I had some eclairs sent over from the bakery. I couldn't resist. I love desserts."

"That's so sweet of you," Anne said. "Can you join us?"

"No, the help doesn't have tea with the guests." Doc's belly wiggled as he walked to hand Anne a cup of tea.

"Oh please. We won't tell Ambrose. I'm dying to hear about this house and the area."

"The house. Well, I can tell you anything you want to know about the house. I've been working here for thirty years."

"That's a long time," Peter said.

"There's not a huge need for butlers anymore, and at my age. I do hope we can add some other staff back though—to get things up to standard. I'm not used to doing all the dusting and preparing food."

"I can help cook. At least while I'm here," Anne offered, her tone was insistent. "I'm used to cooking for a slew of people."

"That's nonsense. You're a guest," Doc scoffed.

"No, for real. I would love to. Sort of to earn my keep. How about until Ambrose gets back, you let me cook. I would love to see what's in a French grocery store anyway. I have to have something to do."

"Well, if you insist, we can try it," Doc said nervously.

Anne blew on her tea and then said, "So, you've worked here for thirty years. Who has lived here?"

"Originally, this estate was owned by Lord and Lady Atquanna, but their dynasty died off from the flu. Then it sat empty for years before the government picked it up. That's when I started working here. We had past government employees mostly residing in it, so it was more formal. But now, with the recession, they had to get it off their expenses, so they put it up for public auction and somehow Ambrose thought it was a good investment."

"You don't?" Peter asked, then bit into an éclair and puckered at the sweetness.

"I do. I love this house, but it's a money pit. Ambrose has a fondness of architecture, but he isn't a fixing man. He hasn't taken to restoring the place as I had hoped."

"He might come around yet," Anne said.

"Maybe," Doc said.

"So, you speak English perfectly," Anne said.

"Yes, I actually lived in the States until I was twelve. Then my parents passed away and I was sent here to live with my great-grandmother."

"I'm sorry to hear about your family," Anne said.

"It's okay. My Grandmother was nice. She had the same affection for pastries as I did, so it worked out." Doc winked at Anne. "Well, I hate to be so chatty. It's not like me. I'll leave you two to visit. I have a whole box of these pastries in the kitchen if you get hungry." He rubbed his hands together like he was trying to warm them up, but you could tell he was just excited about the desserts. "If you would like, Mrs. Arnold, we could take a walk to the bakery in the morning. It's a lovely stroll. You could see if there's something you would like to add to your menu."

"That would be great." Anne smiled at him. After Doc left the room, she turned to Peter and said, "He's so cute; I love him."

"I knew you would." Peter was relieved that Anne was able to meet Doc first because he knew it would ease her nerves about Peter being here and he worried about what she would think about Ambrose. If, he ever returned . . .

CHAPTER SEVENTEEN

*P*eter was sound asleep the next morning when Anne tip-toed into the parlor, holding a tray of butter croissants—her treasure find of the morning—and tea. As she set the tray on the desk, the teacup rattled and woke Peter.

"Mom."

"Yeah."

"You're up already?"

"I couldn't sleep. I was up, and Doc and I went to the bakery. I have a treat for you."

"How was it?" He sat up, leaning against the sofa arm.

"It was fantastic. It was like a cultural experience. So many beautiful desserts that looked like art. I have a feeling I'm going to be carb loading while I'm here." She grinned and steeped Peter's tea for him.

"You've had more cultural experience than I've had since I've been here then." He took the tray from his mom. Biting into his croissant, he felt the texture of butter roll over his tongue. "Man, that's good."

"I've had two already," Anne confessed as she sat next to him on the couch. She smoothed out his blanket. "So, how are you doing?"

"Mom, don't."

"I'm the mom. I want an honest answer."

"The doctors say everything is normal for what my diagnosis is."

"I don't want to know about the doctors. I want to know about what you think."

"I don't think about it. I'm trying to get my project done."

She glared at him, forcing him to look back at her. "I wish you could come back home. If something happens, I would never forgive myself for not being here with you."

"I'm going to be home as soon as I finish my project."

She breathed deeply, then said, "I don't know what you feel inside. I don't know if getting to know Ambrose is your unfinished business. I'm trying hard to understand, but as your mom, it's hard for me to see you go like this. You're so far away."

Peter lifted his arm, and pulled her into a side hug. "I know this is hard for you. I don't really know what I'm doing either, but I promise, if I feel things change, I'll let you know. I wouldn't want to be alone anyway."

"Promise."

"Yeah." Peter squeezed her tighter into their hug.

Anne pulled away first. She sniffed and wiped her nose. "So, the project. How is that?"

"It's good. I burned you a CD. I know you don't do digital music yet." He pointed to a CD on the desk. Anne retrieved it. The cover art was a field of purple lilies, and the title read, "I Should've Asked You First."

"Lilies?"

"That's not the official cover or even final production. It's pretty much just some clip art I found on my computer. I wanted something on there so you would know which one it is. Just add it to your collection."

"I like the photo." Her eyes continued to graze the art. "It sort of makes me sad because I know what the lilies mean to you, but I can't wait to listen to it."

Peter looked down. "Don't be sad. It was therapy to write it. I really do think I've let her go."

"Are you sure?" Anne asked lightly.

"Yeah, I think I'm realizing we were always meant to be best friends." He wrapped his fingers around his opposite hand thumb joint and started to rub. "Everything happened so fast, and I felt like I was losing her friendship. I got confused about what we were to each other."

"I'll admit I'm surprised to hear you say that. I always saw something more in your relationship. Too bad stupid Brad had to come along."

"That pretty much sums it up. Stupid Brad came along."

"You don't have to stop being her friend just because of stupid Brad."

"I do." He raised and lowered his chin. "I can't see him with her anymore. It's just wrong, but she knows if she needs me, I will always be here for her."

"That's a deep realization and very strong of you to let her go like that."

Peter stretched his arms above his head. "So, what else do you want to do today?" He needed to change the subject before the knot in his stomach made him throw up.

"I didn't have any plans. Do you have dialysis this morning?"

"Oh shoot! What time is it?"

"It's after ten."

"Yep. I do. I need to be there for extra labs, too by eleven. Did you want to come with?"

"I wouldn't mind, if it helps you get there faster."

"Sure." Peter swung his legs over the edge of the couch, wincing.

Anne jumped to her feet. "Here, let me rub your hands."

He held his hand out for her. She kneaded his knuckles like she had done every morning when he was little, and surprisingly it was one of the moments he missed the most now he was grown.

"Okay." Anne pushed Peter's chair right up next to the couch. "We need to get moving."

"That we do."

PETER ENJOYED THE WEEK WITH HIS MOM, BUT AS NICE AS IT WAS HAVING her company, he could feel her nervousness and it made him claustrophobic. He was beginning to understand what Gwen had meant when she had told him to get away from people who knew he was sick. On top of her nervousness, Ambrose's return had been delayed and he was only going to get home the night before Anne was scheduled to fly home.

Part of Peter was relieved his mom would have minimal time with him, but the other part was a little annoyed because he wanted her to calm down about him being in France and he knew she would never be able to do that unless, she met and liked Ambrose.

While they waited for Ambrose to arrive, Anne, Doc and Peter sat in the kitchen, stuffing macaroons in their faces. Anne licked her fingers. "I can't believe you eat this stuff every day. I think I'm going to have to start jogging."

"I have crème brûlée in the fridge for after supper," Doc said, then dished up another macaroon for himself.

"It's like torture by deliciousness." Peter pushed his plate away from him. "I can only eat two. It's too sweet for me. I'd rather have a burger."

Doc and Anne both turned their heads, glaring at Peter like he had just sworn at a playground.

"You guys are insane," Peter said. He turned his head away to see Ambrose standing in the doorway. Ambrose had a habit of entering a room silently and then watching the people, like a snake.

"Ambrose, you're back," Peter said.

Doc wiped his fingers off with a towel and stepped back away from the island. "Ambrose, I didn't hear you come back. I was just serving our guests a snack. Would you care for a macaroon?"

Ambrose stepped out of the doorway. "You're not in trouble, Doc. You don't have to follow those stupid self-imposed rules."

Doc's shoulders stiffened even more. "They are not self-imposed. It's etiquette for a butler. Just because you don't require a high standard doesn't mean I don't strive to meet one."

"This is my mom, Anne," Peter said when he caught Ambrose staring at her.

"Hi Anne. Peter said you were visiting. Have you enjoyed your stay?"

"I have. Thank you for letting me stay here. I have been looking forward to meeting you. I've heard so much about you—all good, of course."

Ambrose grinned. "I bet. Don't you talk to the witch?"

Anne's eyebrows furrowed in confusion. "Who?"

"Exa," Ambrose mumbled, reaching across the island, grabbing a handful of macaroons. "These are the best ones in the city," he said as he took a huge bite of one, almost fitting the whole thing into his mouth.

"Here, let me give you a plate." Doc waddled over, setting a plate in front of Ambrose.

Ambrose looked down at it and said, "No, I'm good. Don't need to bother messing that up."

"Well, what's on the agenda tonight, Peter?" Ambrose asked as he crossed the kitchen over to the fridge, opening it with his free hand.

"My mom was hoping we could have dinner together. She leaves tomorrow."

Ambrose found the milk carton, grabbed it, and took a swig.

Anne smiled shyly.

Ambrose looked at her. "What?" he asked.

"Peter does that all the time. You looked just like him when you did that."

Ambrose set the milk carton down. Then he looked back to Peter, and said, "Well, now you know where you get it from."

"I don't think drinking from milk cartons is genetic," Peter said.

"No, maybe not," Anne said. "But you must admit, he looks like you do when he did it. I mean the way he stands and everything. You could be twins."

Peter stared awkwardly at Ambrose. Part of him wished his mom wouldn't be as vocal about her observations, as they embarrassed him. The other part of him longed to hear stuff like that: it was a self-discovery he didn't even know he needed.

LATER THAT NIGHT, AMBROSE MET PETER AND ANNE AT A RESTAURANT HE suggested called Bon Appétit, a locally owned café close to the house.

"I think I better have some protein." Anne read the menu. "I've exceeded my carbohydrate limit for the year."

Ambrose grinned. "Doc has a thing for white flour, and he knows how to make you his partner in crime. He's like a giant kid when it comes to sugar."

"I find it endearing. I will miss him for sure," Anne said.

"You should try the steak tartare." Ambrose grinned daringly at Anne.

"Or not," Peter said.

"What's wrong with it?" Anne questioned. "Steak sounds good."

"It's raw steak," Peter replied.

"Oh yuck. I can't eat that. What else is there?" Overwhelmed by her menu, Anne missed the leadership of Doc, who always knew exactly what she would like.

"Have you ever had the James Roper?" Ambrose asked. "It's what the French call putting an egg on a ham and cheese sandwich."

Anne wrinkled her nose. "That doesn't sound good either."

"So, I guess, I'm not going to be able to convince you to order the escargot. It's excellent here," Ambrose said before taking a drink of water.

"You know, Peter, I guess I'm starting to see how you would miss hamburgers," Anne said.

"Or become a carb addict," Peter added.

"How about just a simple roast chicken with wine sauce," Ambrose suggested. "It's excellent as well."

"That might be okay," Anne agreed. "I can't find anything else that sounds normal. I'll try that."

"Then you'll have more room for dessert," Peter joked as he ordered the same thing his mom did.

"No, I'm done with sugar for a month!" Anne folded her menu and gave it to the waiter. Ambrose ordered something in French. The waiter came back with a bottle of red wine and poured it into Ambrose's glass. Anne and Peter both declined a glass. "So, tell me, Ambrose," Anne started, "what it is about France that keeps you here? Don't you get homesick?"

"I don't really have anything left in the States and the people there are so fanatical about celebrities it became hard for me to do simple tasks like going out for a drink or even standing in my yard."

"You don't get recognized here?"

"No, they recognize me, but they don't care."

"Really?" Anne turned her head toward Peter and asked, "Have you been recognized while you were here?"

He shrugged his shoulders. "I haven't gone anywhere except doctors' appointments, so I guess I didn't even notice."

Ambrose continued, "I was visiting here years ago, and I was out walking around downtown, no one said anything. Then, finally when I was getting ready to leave a pub, I said something to a bartender, and he said he noticed who I was, and he thought most everyone in there did as well, but they didn't care. I knew then I had to move here. It's really the only way to live a semi-normal life."

"So you buy a castle? That's not a good way to blend in," Peter said.

"Again, the French don't care. And who wouldn't want to live in a castle? So, my turn to ask you a question." Ambrose leaned back in his chair. "What have you heard about me from the witch?"

Anne looked to Peter, and then they both looked back at Ambrose. Peter timidly spoke, "She didn't talk about you much. We were friends for a long time before I knew she was married. I had to pry your name out of her."

"I won't say much because I know you guys are friends, but in case you haven't noticed the gal's crazy psycho, and if she did tell you anything about me, I would hesitate to believe it." Ambrose took a sip of his wine. "I don't know, I guess in hindsight, we barely know each other. It's been years since we had a real conversation."

Peter looked down at the candle glowing in the center of the table. It was an uncomfortable conversation, and he didn't want to meddle. "I think women are supposed to drive men nuts," he joked to try to lighten the mood. "So, are we still going into the studio tomorrow to finish our recording?"

Ambrose frowned and was about to say something, but instead blurted out, "Here's the food coming over. I'm starving." The waiter handed out the plates.

"It looks wonderful." Anne set her napkin on her lap.

Peter glared at Ambrose. He knew Ambrose had deliberately dodged his question. There was something about Ambrose that was bugging him, so that night after dinner when Peter was alone in the parlor, he called Exa.

"Pe ta."

"Hey, how's it going?"

"It's going okay. It's good to hear your voice. I've been thinking about you. What time is it?"

"Almost ten."

"Yeah, it's dinner time here," Exa said. "Is your mom still over there?"

"Yeah, she's leaving tomorrow in the morning."

"What's wrong, Pe ta? Are you in trouble?"

"No, I don't think so." He swallowed hard, and then went right to the heart of his concern. "I wanted to know more about Ambrose. I just don't see him being like you said."

"That's his MO. He sucks you in and then when you let your guard down, he will get you."

"I don't see it."

"What happened? There must be something bothering you, or you wouldn't call me."

"Nothing." He knew it was a lie, but he didn't want to confess all of his apprehensives. "We've been getting along."

"Your mom said you were staying with him to try to get to know him or something. Whose idea was that?"

"His. I wouldn't invite myself over here."

"Maybe if you are feeling weird, it's time to leave. Just come home with your mom in the morning. It's not that big of a deal."

"I would, but I have to finish this project first."

"What project?"

"We are recording a song together. Something Ambrose wanted to do. I think maybe he wanted to get to know me."

"That doesn't sound like him," she said, sounding concerned. "He doesn't care about anyone, but himself. Did you do it?"

"Yeah, well, we still have one more part to record."

Exa was quiet and then said, "I don't know what the deal was, but take my advice, as soon as you are done recording, leave."

"Well, I can't do that exactly."

"Why not?"

"Because the song was my part of the deal. He has his own part he needs to hold up. I can't leave until he does that."

"I don't like what you are telling me. I thought I warned you about him. You can't make a deal with him. If you are waiting for him to hold up a deal, you can forget it. It will never happen."

"You sound so cynical."

"I prefer to say 'realistic.' Trust me, I know. Get away from him."

"I wish I could, but I can't. At this point, I'm invested."

"I'm not joking. There is no investment worth hanging out for. Cut your loss and go home with your mom tomorrow."

"I don't know."

"Why did you call me if you aren't going to listen to me?"

"I guess I was hoping you'd tell me something different."

"And now that I'm not, you don't care to listen to the advice I have?"

"It's not that I don't care to listen to it. I am listening, but I can't take your advice."

"I don't know what else to say then if you are not going to listen. I hope your mom can talk some sense into you before she leaves."

"I think she likes him."

"He does that to people. He's a charmer at first—before he ruins your life."

"I don't see him being that bad, but if I do I guess I'll leave."

"It might be too late then."

"I appreciate your concern, but it's getting late here, and I want to take my mom in the morning so I better go."

"Alright. Take care of yourself."

"I will." Peter ended the call. He had been tired when he came into the room, but now he was wide awake. The person Exa talked about and the person he saw just didn't match up.

The next day after Anne reluctantly left Peter at the airport to fly home, Peter returned to the house, ready to get recording so he could follow in her direction. He noticed immediately that Ambrose wasn't home.

"Hey, Doc, did Ambrose say where he went?" Doc was stretching to clean a mirror in the hallway, and as he stretched, his belly pressed against the wall, sandwiching it as he tried to get closer to the wall to reach higher.

"He said something about drinks at a pub. Were you going to meet him?"

"Not for drinks, but we had plans to record our stuff this afternoon. Should I text him?"

Doc lowered his hand, shaking his arm as his shoulder had gotten stiff. "I wouldn't. He seemed like he needed to blow off some steam. Maybe wait to see when he comes back."

"Really? Because I find it rude he would go drinking when we have plans. I have plans. I need to get on with this project." Peter's voice was irritated, but Doc didn't seem to notice. He was running a dust cloth around the floor trim. "I can't believe he hasn't hired a housekeeper yet. He can't expect you to do all the work of like six people," Peter ranted.

Doc was now on his knees as he scooted along the wall, wiping. "I can't say anything right now because I don't have anywhere else to go." Sweat beaded down his brow as he huffed out the words.

"I seriously can't watch you do this. It's painful." Peter grabbed a broom from Doc's pile. Then he pushed forward on the controls to his wheelchair, driving the chair along the wall with the broom wiping the trim. "This is way less work," he said, pleased with his innovation.

Doc sat up, admiring Peter's industriousness. "It does work faster when it's powered by a motor. I do think you should just let me do it. It's too much for you."

"I don't have anything else to do, and I know the reason you're dusting everything is because I'm allergic to it, so I might as well help you." Peter lifted the broom and moved to the adjacent wall.

"You know, I have one of those dusters. I bet it will slide better on that. Let me grab it." He left eagerly, excited for the help.

The rest of the afternoon they motor dusted anything within Peter's reach. It was efficient and completely entertaining.

"Hey, you guys look like you're having fun," Ambrose said, leaning against the doorframe and pulling off his shoes.

"It's been a laid-back afternoon while I was waiting for you." Peter glared at him.

"Waiting for me? Oh, that's too bad. I didn't know." He threw both his shoes in the corner and turned on his heel to go up the stairs.

"We had an appointment to finish our project today. Did you forget?"

"It's been a long day. I just need to rest now. We can talk more in the morning." He spoke as he walked right by Peter and went up the stairs.

Peter wanted to chew him out for blowing him off, but he didn't know if that was a good idea either because he still needed his kidney. He was completely at the mercy of this guy, and the longer this project drug out, the more Peter saw about Ambrose he didn't trust. All he wanted to do was have the operation and go home.

The next morning, Peter made sure he was available when Ambrose came downstairs, breezed into the kitchen, looked at Peter, and said, "Hey, bud, what ya got going on today?"

"I'm waiting on you."

Ambrose reached into the cupboard and grabbed a bowl and then cereal from another cupboard. "Oh yeah, about that, I don't think I'm going to be able to hang today, because I got some guys to meet." He poured the cereal into the bowl.

Peter wanted to be composed, but he was losing his patience. He had waited weeks for something that should take a day to get done. "That's cool if you have plans, but can we set a time for us to get this done?"

"We'll get to it. What's the big rush?"

"I'm sort of on a time line, which now that I have brought that up, we should probably talk about it. You haven't gone into the doctor to get your tests done, and that takes time. Do you want me to schedule you a pre-op with my doctor? He's super busy and is booked out like two months."

"I'm not so sure I can have the surgery right now." Ambrose shoved a spoon of cereal into his mouth and then said, "I have all these projects going on. I wouldn't want to be put out and the holidays are coming up."

"Since when do you care about the holidays?"

"It's just a lot to ask from someone." Ambrose's words were muffled as he spoke while chomping on cereal.

That stung. Peter didn't know what to say. After a few moments of silence except for Ambrose chomping with his mouth open—an annoying habit that gave Peter another reason to believe he didn't have the maturity past a twelve-year-old—Ambrose looked up. "Alright, I'll make you a deal. After Christmas, I'll go in and get all the tests done, and we can get serious about this thing."

"Christmas? That's another two months away. You're not even religious."

"No, but I know this is going to be hard on my body. It's a lot to ask, and I want to have some time to get used to the idea." Ambrose finished the last of his cereal. Peter couldn't even face him. *We already made a deal before*. Nothing felt right about this deal, but he didn't have a choice. Ambrose was his only hope.

CHAPTER EIGHTEEN

ANNE

*W*hen Peter didn't come home for the holidays, Anne tried to remain calm. She waited until Paul and Tane were on break, so they could help with Shiloh, Johnny, and Macey. She had bigger concerns on her mind, so she flew across the ocean to face them.

This time when she stepped off the plane, Peter and Doc were both waiting for her. The sight of Peter's emaciated, pasty, white body shocked her. She tried not to stare, but his health had deteriorated greatly in the last months. As they walked out of the airport, Doc wheeled Peter's chair in silence. It was obvious Doc was with Peter not out of a desire to greet Anne, but out of necessity because Peter was too weak to make the short trip alone. Anne was kicking herself inside about waiting so long to visit. Now after seeing Peter in this condition, she resigned herself to the fact she was not leaving France alone. She had to convince Peter to come home, even as a last resort.

Once inside the house and after much slow, painstaking cooperation between the three of them to get Peter inside and comfortable in his chair, Anne sat with Peter in the parlor--neither one of them resting.

Instead of them feasting on pastries like her last visit, Doc wheeled in a cart with soup for the two of them to share while Peter rested in bed. Doc had a different energy this visit. Instead of being a jolly guy on a sugar rush, he was sober and attentive. He left the tray in the room and closed the door, giving them privacy.

All Anne wanted to do was beg him to come home, but she knew that would only have the opposite effect on his stubborn mind. Peter didn't have the energy to talk, as the trip to the airport wore him out. His eye lids were heavy, and he was drifting.

"Here, can I help you eat?" She lifted the ladle out of the crock, pouring soup into a bowl.

"Sure."

She scooted closer to him and scooped up a small spoon of the broth, blew on it, and held the spoon to his mouth while he slurped it up like a child. The sight of him eating from her like a toddler, broke her heart, but she kept a strong face with a pleasant smile as she counted the spoonfuls he ate. Just nine spoonfuls of soup and his head began to get heavy, and he leaned back against the couch.

"Do you need to rest?"

"Yeah, I'm tired."

Anne set the bowl down and grabbed his blanket, tucking it around him. She pulled a pillow out from behind him and fluffed it up for his head to rest on it. It took only a moment and his breathing slowed, indicating he was sleeping. Anne stood watching over him, holding her breath unable to believe she had spent the last twenty minutes caring for him like a baby.

She decided to sleep by Peter's side because she knew she would never get any rest upstairs on the second floor with him so far away. But first, she needed answers. She grabbed the food tray and carried it out to the kitchen, looking for Doc along the way. He sat in the kitchen at the table, staring out the window with a cup of tea in front of him.

"May I get you anything else?" He stood upon her entering.

"No, I'm fine. I wanted to chat." She sat on a stool across from him. "I have to ask, how long has he been like this?"

Doc sat back down. "It's been a gradual thing. I didn't notice at first, but when Ambrose took off this last time, it seems like you can mark the weeks he has been gone. Each week that we don't hear from him, Peter just sinks further into his own world."

"I really wish someone would have called me. I can't leave him like this. I have to take him home with me. Why is he waiting around on Ambrose anyway?"

Doc's face flushed. "I shouldn't tell you, but I think he made a deal with Ambrose. I've heard them arguing. I think Ambrose promised him a kidney. Peter doesn't want to leave here because he feels like if he leaves without a kidney then he is leaving to, you know, give up."

Anne sighed. "I was afraid of something like this. I never asked him much, and he always made it sound like they never talked about the kidney, but part of me was wondering if Ambrose wasn't bullying him into staying here. It's just not like Peter to be so far from family, especially in his condition. Who is taking care of him? Just you?"

"I do my best. This last month has been the worst, and his dialysis doctor recommended he get a home health nurse to check on him in the middle of the week. She comes and checks his vitals, sets up his meds, helps with showering, but even she can't do much."

"This is going to stop. I don't care about where Ambrose is. I'm taking him home. I was scheduled to stay until the end of the week, but I'm going to see if I can move my flight up and add a seat for him. Do you have his doctor's number?"

"I do. But for what it's worth, I know Ambrose is due home in the next day or two. Would you want to wait to see him?"

"I honestly don't know if I have anything to say to him. This has gone way too far as it is."

"Let me know what your plans are, and I will try to help. In the meantime, you need to rest. I'll have breakfast in the parlor for the both of you in the morning when Peter wakes up."

"God bless you, Doc. You don't have to do all this, but I appreciate you." She reached over to hug him, and as she embraced him, he froze.

"It's my pleasure. I've gotten a little fond of the kid. I'm going to miss having him around, but I'll be relieved to know he's with family."

"It's wonderful you are here for him."

"Say, Anne . . ."

"Hmm?"

"I know it's none of my business, but he doesn't say much, and I was wondering, what happens if Ambrose doesn't give him a kidney?"

Her throat got dry and she swallowed before mustering up her words. "Peter wouldn't be here if Ambrose wasn't his last resort."

"How do you mean?"

"He needs a kidney, and because of his disability and his frailty, it needs to come from family. Exa wasn't a match. Ambrose is the only blood relative he has who is a match."

Doc looked down at his knuckles. "How does he know he's a match? I don't think Ambrose has done any tests."

Anne pursed her lips in annoyance. "That's discouraging to hear. I would have hoped he'd gotten his tests done months ago, but I guess I'm not surprised. We know he's the right blood type because Exa wasn't."

"You need an O-negative?"

Anne looked surprised. "How did you know?"

"Ah, I saw Ambrose's blood on a record somewhere. Maybe when I was cleaning."

Anne furrowed her brow as her mom instinct alerted her to something in Doc's tone. "Hmm."

"Well, I need to make my last nightly rounds, unless I can get you anything?" He looked back over at her, with a helpful gaze.

Anne's brain was racing. She wasn't ready for Doc to leave. "Umm." She cleared her throat.

"Yes, what do you need?"

"It's just, how much do you know about Ambrose?"

"How do you mean?"

"You work for him. It never dawned on me before to ask, but does he have any other family or any other kids? I guess, right now I'm thinking Ambrose isn't wanting to help Peter, and it sure would be nice to learn he had another kid with his same blood type."

Doc studied her face and then sat back down. After moments of silence, he softly said, "I blew my cover, didn't I?"

Anne stared back at him, grinning.

He rubbed the back of his neck and grimaced. "Did you have a clue?"

"Not at all, but when the thought entered my head, it was the only thing that made sense. Why would you know his blood type? So, you're his . . .?"

"Dad." There was a twinkle in Doc's eyes that confirmed his words to be true.

Anne grinned teasingly like she had solved a crime. "You're not just a butler."

"No, I'm a butler, and my career has been in this house. When it came up for sale and I was about to lose my job, Ambrose purchased it and moved in. Pretty much to drive me insane."

Anne giggled. "He calls you Doc?"

"In his youth when he was learning to speak, that's how it came out, instead of Dad. It always just stuck. Of course, back then, I was still his hero." Doc's eyes beamed with pride.

"A true term of endearment then. And we all miss the days when our kids thought we woke up thirty minutes before they did so we could hang the sun just for them."

"That is the complete truth."

"So you guys are close now that you live together?"

"Nah, but it just sort of happened, and it is what is. I do like seeing him regularly." Doc nervously scratched the back of his head. "He's not who he used to be, but he's still a part of me and I like being able to keep an eye on him."

"I can't see someone with Ambrose's personality being a child of yours. You're so kind."

Doc looked down.

"Sorry." Anne covered her mouth in embarrassment. "I didn't mean it like that. It's just you know, he's a little rougher."

"It's okay. I know what you meant. You know the biz." He shrugged his shoulders. "It's the industry. The fame ruined him. He wasn't always like that. He was a sweet little boy for the first part of his life."

"His mom? Is she?"

Doc's facial lines softened into a small grin. "She passed on to live with the good Lord when Ambrose was ten."

"I'm sorry to hear that. It never dawned on me to even ask if you had a family. Now I feel foolish."

"It's quite alright. I'm not one for sharing my personal business with people."

"So you knew Peter was your grandson this whole time?"

He nodded.

"I wish I would have known. It might've eased my mom nerves a little to know you were looking out for him the whole time."

"Forgive me for not saying anything?"

"Why keep it a secret?"

"Ambrose didn't want me to say anything to Peter. I guess as dumb as it is, my loyalty is still with Ambrose, even though now as I sit here, I can feel a protective pull to Peter."

"Peter has that effect on people." Anne winked at him. "Thanks for taking care of our boy."

"It was my pleasure. I got to know a grandson I never thought I'd have the chance to get to know. You did a wonderful job raising him."

"I had a lot of grace for that one." She took a deep breath, and then continued, "I have to ask . . ."

He shook his head. "It breaks my heart to come so far in this conversation to have to tell you, but no. I know what you're thinking, but my beautiful Georgina, God rest her soul, was the O."

Anne let out a depleting breath. In a tiny voice, she said, "Okay. Thank you."

"Boy wouldn't that be somethin'? A true miracle of events if it could be any different."

Anne wiped at the edge of her eye. "It's okay. Thank you for being honest." She leaned in, embracing Doc once more before saying goodnight and going to bed.

CHAPTER NINETEEN

Two days passed, and Peter felt like he was a mime who was stuck in his imaginary box while other people watched him pretend to go about his day, mimicking what normal life used to be.

He stared blankly at his plate offering him a plain croissant, something he normally would have loved to dip in his hot chocolate, but the thought of eating gagged him. Looking across the table at his mom's plate, he noticed she hadn't touched anything either.

Anne cleared her throat. "Would you like to come with me for a walk through the gardens? I can tell spring is finally waking up the yard."

"Maybe later."

"What's with all the tired faces?" Ambrose stood in the kitchen doorway, looking tan and fresh.

Peter's head jerked back like he was suddenly awakened from the longest daydream. "You're back."

"Anne, I wasn't expecting to see you here." Ambrose reached out to shake her hand.

"I hope it's okay." She forced a smile as she extended her hand.

"Absolutely, we have room for the whole family, if they want to come."

Doc spoke, "Did you need help with luggage or can I get you something to drink?"

"How about a screwdriver. This room needs an energy lift. You people look terrible. What's been going on while I've been gone?" He pulled up a stool and sat.

Anne spoke, "We are having breakfast and planning our day."

"Cool. Oh Doc, can you get me an ice pack?" Ambrose asked.

Doc obediently took an ice pack out of the freezer and grabbed a towel to wrap around it. "Anything else?" he asked when he handed it over.

"Nah, this should help my shoulder. Yesterday, when I was in London, I was getting my back tattoos touched up, and there was this woman there who was getting her baby's ear pierced. I don't know how old he was, maybe like this big." Ambrose held his hands apart about two feet. "Anyway, this little boy had a three-inch mohawk. That kid is going to be a stud." He laughed like he hadn't been sober for days.

"I gotta go to dialysis." Peter said flatly as he didn't have the stomach to listen to Ambrose's stories. He pushed his chair back from the table.

"I'll help you." Anne followed him.

Peter heard Ambrose loudly joking to Doc about the flight attendant on his last plane ride as he wheeled himself down the hall and out the front door.

"At least he made it back finally," Anne said, softly.

"Yeah, I guess."

"Is he hard to get along with?"

Peter scanned the street, looking for Leo. "There he is. Just pulling through the gate. Are you coming with me?"

"I was planning to."

"Okay, that's fine. Ah, Ambrose, you know, when you see him, he's nice and friendly, so it's not hard to get along with him, but he seems to be like one of those people who gets distracted."

"Do you think he's distracted or do you think it's an act to get out of his responsibility?"

"What do you mean?"

"You arranged a deal when you arrived, and he hasn't taken even the first step toward fulfilling that agreement. From my experience dealing with people, his intentions are probably not to fulfill it."

Peter flung his hand out in question. "Why are you saying this?"

"I don't mean to make you upset, but sometimes people disappoint you, and sometimes they flat out screw you over." Her lips frowned, and she added, "I worry about his intentions. Frankly, the way he has put you off is cruel, considering what is at stake."

Leo pulled the car up in front of them and got out, greeting them with a smile. He opened the back door for Anne and helped Peter into the front seat. He wheeled Peter's chair back to Doc, who was watching by the door.

"Mom, I know you're worried, and to be honest, I was too." Peter craned his neck as far to the side as he could to talk to her. "I didn't know when Ambrose was coming back, but I think now that he's here it's a good sign. I'll talk to him tonight."

"Good. I can help you if you want, but we need to talk too. If he says no or puts you off, I want you to come home with me—soon."

Peter's eyes had begun to burn since sitting in the car. He saw the air vents had a film of dust on them. He ran his fingers along the plastic slants, wiping them clean. Anne dug in her purse for a tissue. "Here." She handed it to him. "You're going to make it worse by getting it all over your hands."

"It's just dust. Probably what I will be before I make it home." He didn't even bother to look back at his mom when he said it because he knew her heart was breaking, but at this point it felt like better sooner than later.

LATER, DOC BROUGHT PETER A TRAY WITH LEMON WATER AND HOT WATER for tea, which Peter ignored. He dropped his duffle bag onto the couch and searched for the few material items he had brought with him. "Are you packing?" Anne stood in the doorway.

"Yep."

"Do I need to know something?"

"I'm going to talk to Ambrose tonight. I sort of think I already know the answer, but either way I'm not staying in this house anymore. If he says, yes, I'll get a hotel. I just can't stand seeing him procrastinate."

"If he says no?"

Peter looked up. "Then, I'll go home with you."

Anne sunk down onto the armchair facing him. "Okay, I can start looking at some tickets. Maybe we can fly standby. Or maybe we won't need to." She flashed an optimistic grin. He knew it was fake, but he loved her for it. She continued, "Well, I guess I can make myself useful. I'll get a hotel lined up too, just in case. And my bags packed."

"Don't act so excited."

"You know me. I'm a planner."

He zipped his bag. "I'm ready. I don't see the point in dragging this out. I'm going to find him."

She placed a reassuring hand on his arm and said, "You're doing the right thing."

"It's time." He wheeled his chair out of the parlor to find Doc, which wasn't hard because he stood at the front door, talking to an old lady who looked like a street-beggar.

"Hey," Peter said as he wheeled up behind him.

"What can I get you?" Doc turned around and slightly closed the door, blocking the lady.

"Can you help me visit Ambrose? I don't think I can make it up the stairs by myself."

"Ambrose has been hanging out in the south tower. It's five flights of stairs."

"I don't care. I just can't wait for him any longer. Can you help me?"

"I can try. It's quite a hike; the last flight of stairs is basically a ladder. Why don't you let me text him, and have him come down?"

"No, I don't want him to do me any more favors than I need him to. Please, Doc."

"I guess I'm up for a challenge." He half smiled.

"I have my cane, too." Peter took it from his lap, and leaned on it to help himself lift out of his chair. Doc came up on the opposite side, wrapped Peter's arm around his shoulders, and hoisted him up.

"This is going to be an interesting journey." Doc winked at him and they moved toward the stairs. "Okay, you give me your cane and I'll carry it in this hand," he said as he reached for the cane with his right hand. "You hold onto the banister with your other hand."

"Oh wait, what about that lady?" Peter asked.

"Oomph, I forgot. My mind is scattered these days. Wait here, I'll tell her to come back." Doc left the landing and opened the door, revealing no one there. He stuck his head out and looked both ways. "She left."

"Who was she?" Peter reached out for Doc's shoulder to reassume their climbing positions. They set off at a good pace, making it up the front stairs with little fatigue. "She said, 'she was a relative of Lady Atquanna's.' I guess she used to spend holidays here when she was a little girl. She must be a hundred. She wanted a tour. I was going to invite her in because I'd love to learn more about the house—if she had any memories. Maybe she'll come back."

They headed down the hall to find the back staircase, which they could take to get them up the next two stories. "She would be neat to talk to," Peter said. "So, Doc," Peter continued as they started the second set of steps.

"Are you doing okay?"

"Yeah, I'm fine, but I need to tell you I'm leaving tonight."

"You are?"

"Yeah, getting a hotel with my mom. I need some space."

Doc's eyes widened. "That seems sudden."

"I think it should have happened a while ago, but I needed someone to remind me to be strong."

"You got the reminder?"

"I did."

"Well, it's going to be quiet here without you. Let me know how I can help with your departure."

"I don't think there is much you can do. Unless you can find me a kidney." Peter forced the joke to lighten the mood as he felt himself getting sad. He never expected to make a friend in Doc, but months of having Doc care for him like a small child forced him to attach in a way that was comforting.

"Phew," Doc said as they reached the end of that staircase. "Do you want to rest or keep going?"

"Might as well get it over." The little muscle tone Peter had was giving way and forcing Doc to do all the work.

"Alright, let's give it one last push." Doc opened the wooden door to the attic-like stairs leading to the tower lookout. "I don't really trust these stairs. I think they are original to the house." Each board creaked in agony as their weight was applied.

"I didn't know they would be this bad—or steep. I should have listened to you when you offered to have Ambrose come down."

"We're not turning back now." Doc's words came out in huffs of breath. "Okay, six more steps." Doc held his breath as he boosted Peter once again up the steps. At the top of the narrow landing was a door. "I'll wait on the steps for you." He handed Peter his cane.

"Hopefully, this doesn't take too long." Peter turned the doorknob and stuck his cane onto the bottom of the door, pushing it open.

CHAPTER TWENTY

"Hey, big Pete." Ambrose lounged on a window bench.

"Hi." Peter closed the door, leaned on his cane, and walked to a bench opposite of Ambrose. He wasn't scared of heights, but the combination of the wind and being alone with Ambrose made for a tepid environment. Originally, when the tower was built, it was part of the roof, but the previous owners had enclosed it, making it look more like an enclosed patio with window screens. Higher than any structure close by, the wind was fierce.

"How'd you get up here?"

"Doc helped me. It was a lot farther than I thought." There was a bottle next to Ambrose's foot. The wind wafted the smell of whatever Ambrose was drinking over, making Peter turn his head from the stench. Then he looked out over the city and said, "It's a nice view." He saw a lot of buildings in gray hues that mostly had red roofs. The modesty of incomes was reflected in the box-like architecture and plain landscaping.

"I love it up here. I'm going to add a bar for entertaining."

"That will be nice."

Ambrose took a swig from his bottle, and leaned back against the screened window with the bottle braced against his leg.

"Should you be leaning against that?" Peter asked.

"It's fine. It's not like I'm a fatty."

Peter sighed. *It's now or never.* "So, I'm going to call my part of our recording project wrapped up. I know you said you wanted to spend a day with the studio musicians, but that was months ago, and I need to move on." *You're probably too drunk to be having this conversation right now, but I don't have any more time to waste,* Peter thought.

Ambrose closed one eye as he focused on Peter. "We made a cool song."

"I think it turned out well."

"Yeah, it's a cool song . . . for your last one."

Peter's chest tightened. "What?"

"You know what I mean." Ambrose took another swig of his bottle and leaned his head back against the screen, closing his eyes.

"I'm not sure if I do. If you mean it to sound how it came off, it seems sort of morbid."

"But, it is morbid. Your situation has always been morbid."

"That's frank. I don't think this is a good time for us to be talking. You seem drunk."

"Nah, I'm just buzzed. I know what I'm sayin'."

"Do you?"

"Yeah, I do. What do you want me to lie to you and say everything's going to be fine? That I'm your daddy and I'll save you." Ambrose took a swig of his drink, but laughed, causing him to choke. He coughed, holding his hand to his mouth. "Ah, excuse me. Good stuff. You want some?" He held the bottle towards Peter.

"No, I'm okay."

"You don't drink, do you?"

Peter shook his head. He was beyond uncomfortable with this conversation, but he had a plan, and his mom was waiting.

"You're such a good boy. Poor Peter." He snickered. "Everyone loves and wants to save poor Peter." He sat up straighter, leaning forward. "Do you wanna know somethin'?"

"What?"

"I don't want to save poor Peter."

A cold sweat frosted Peter's low back despite the wind blowing through the room like a tunnel.

Ambrose stood up, wobbling from the booze. Grabbing the ledge to steady himself, wickedly laughing, he said, "Look, now I'm walking like you! Hey, catch me or I'm going to fall." He stumbled closer to Peter.

Peter stood, and said, "Doc's waiting inside. I think he needs to help get you to bed." Peter gripped his cane, resenting it the whole time. Ambrose was acting like the school kids who used to tease him. He knew to block it out, but it stung. Peter cracked the door open to see Doc huddled nervously on the step. His cheeks were blushing, confirming he could hear their whole conversation.

"I'll help him down, but I'm not leaving you up here alone. I texted your mom to come up here, but she's not responding," Doc said. "I'll run down to grab her."

"He's way gone." Peter held his hand like he was holding a cup and tipped it to his mouth.

"Stupid drunk. I wish we could steal his kidney from him while he sleeps. He doesn't take care of it." Doc had a moisture to his eyes but tried to hide it by looking away when he left to descend the stairs.

Peter looked back at Ambrose, who was now standing on the bench. "Wow, dude, you'd better sit down." Peter reached out toward him, helping him to sit.

"You're so boring." Ambrose leaned back, but mostly just fell over to his side on top of the bench. "I mean it. What do you do for fun?"

Peter ignored his taunts, glancing back to the empty doorway.

"I gotta tell you somethin'," Ambrose slurred his words together.

"Don't bother. You're not making any sense." Peter's legs were still fatigued from the climb up the stairs. He sat back on the bench, trying to tune out Ambrose as he waited impatiently for Doc's return.

"Your music sucks. Who listens to classical music anyway?"

Peter bit his lip, hard.

"Do you know why I wanted you to record with me?"

"Why?" Peter asked in the tiniest of voices, not sure why he was engaging in this punishment.

"Because I knew you were gonna be takin' a dirt nap, and I wanted to be the one person who had your last professionally recorded song. People go nuts for artists after they die. Can you imagine how much that's going to be worth?" He flung his head back, chuckling the cruelest of sounds Peter had ever heard.

"You really are who Exa said you are." Peter stared at him, seeing the evil man for who he was.

"Don't bring up that witch. You're gonna ruin my buzz. Oh, there's my bottle." When Ambrose had tipped over in his drunken stupor, he fell on his bottle. Distracted by the thought of another drink, he forgot the conversation and pulled his bottle out, taking another swig. When he was done, he set his focus on Peter. He closed one eye, then the other. Then he opened them both. "You sure are ugly."

Doc and Anne's footsteps could be heard outside the door. Relieved, Peter stood, gripping his cane with a shaky hand—his anger was boiling over.

"Hey, honey," Anne said as she wrapped her arm around Peter's waist, steering him away.

"Let's give them a minute to get ahead, and then I will help you down." Peter heard Doc tell Ambrose.

Ambrose called to Peter, who was now on the staircase. "Not only are you ugly, but you're gonna die, because I'm never giving you a kidney. When you die, I'm going to sell that demo for a billion smackaroonis!"

Anne caught her breath in a gasp as she shot Peter an alarmed look. "Ignore it, Mom. He's drunk. We can go home."

CHAPTER TWENTY-ONE

*P*eter wore his earbuds, listening to Internet radio on his phone while he sat next to his mom at the airport gate. They were on the list for stand-by to go home. If they didn't get on this flight, they had confirmed seats on a flight that was leaving in the morning and a hotel confirmation to get them through the night.

Anne munched on a bag of airport pretzels. "I don't ever think I'll look at carbs the same way again."

Peter adjusted his ear bud so he could hear his mom. "Huh?"

"When you've dined on French baguettes and croissants, it's impossible to find pleasure in processed pretzels."

"You're going to have to adjust."

"I don't think I will. Maybe I'll try that new ketogenic diet everyone's talking about."

"I could go on a diet that says you can eat all the bacon you want."

"Can you really eat as much as you want? That seems weird."

"Look it up."

"I think I will." Anne pulled out her phone, tapped on her Internet icon, and searched for the diet. Peter replaced his earbud, looked down to his phone, and noticed a text message from Doc: *"Peter, can you call me? It's urgent."*

He dialed Doc, and placed the phone next to his ear, listening to it ring.

"Peter," Doc answered the phone.

"Hey, did you want me to call you?"

"Don't get on a plane."

"I know it stinks, but I can't stay here."

"Don't leave the country. There's been an accident. It's Ambrose."

"And I care why?"

"Because it's bad, and the doctors don't think he will live. He fell out of the tower. One of the window screens gave out."

"What?" He froze from shock. "How'd that happen?"

"I don't know. I tried to help him down, but he refused to let me. So I left. I was in my room when I heard him scream. I was too late. He broke his neck, smashed part of his skull, and he has uncontrolled internal bleeding. Doctors said he's probably not going to make it through the night."

"I don't believe it." Peter held his chest with one hand. "That's terrible."

"But, Peter, it isn't," Doc's voice was quietly respectful, but he continued, "his kidneys are fine. He landed on his head."

"What are you saying?"

"I'm saying, they are talking about harvesting his organs. Get your butt in here and get in line."

"I um, don't think it works like that."

"I don't know how it usually works, but this is how it's going to work. Call your dialysis doctor. He works at the same hospital. Just come down here!"

"I, I can't believe it."

"Don't waste too much time being stunned, and get your butt down here! I gotta go be with him, but I'll be waiting for you."

"I don't know. It seems sort of . . . wrong. I'll think about it. Bye." Peter ended the call, and glanced over at his mom, who had obviously been eavesdropping on his conversation. Her eyebrow was raised, ready to listen. "There's been an accident," Peter said slowly.

"Yeah."

"It's like a freak of nature or something, but Ambrose fell from that tower, and now he's at the hospital dying, and they are getting ready to harvest his organs."

Anne gasped, covering her mouth with her hand. "Oh my word, that's terrible. Are they sure it's that bad?"

"Doc seems to think so."

"I didn't have a good feeling when we left him up there. He was so drunk."

Peter looked sideways at his mom, because he knew she would get excited about the next part. "There's something else."

"What?"

"Doc has reason to believe his kidneys are fine."

"Is that possible?" she whispered.

"I don't know."

"Is it honorable for us to be having this conversation right now?" Anne looked around the room like she thought she would get in trouble from someone. "This could be the answer to my prayers," she whispered.

"But, Mom, it's sort of creepy. I mean the timing and all."

"No, it's perfect." Anne picked up her purse. "Let's get a cab. We're going to the hospital." She ran behind Peter's wheelchair, removing the breaks from his wheels, and pushed him into motion before he had a chance to protest. She pushed with one hand and held her cell phone in the other. "I'm calling your dad to see what he thinks. You call your doctor. If there is a way for us to get that kidney, I'm going to find it."

CHAPTER TWENTY-TWO

Six weeks later, Peter wheeled his chair on American soil while reaping the benefits of a successful kidney transplant surgery. The last weeks had been a blur. All he knew was he was given a second chance at life, and he wasn't going to waste it.

He turned his key in the front door at his parents' house. Anne waited beside him as he opened the door to see the rest of his family waiting in the living room yelling out a huge, "Surprise!" Only he wasn't surprised. He knew his family too well, and he knew they would make a big deal out of his homecoming.

He was greeted by the scent he always knew as home. It was a mixture of Anne's vanilla candles, and her all-natural cleaning spray scented with grapefruit essential oil. He was home. It was such a gift to be here and to know he had the biggest gift of all—time.

After only a couple hours, Peter became too exhausted to stay up and he honestly couldn't think of a time in his life when he was more excited to lie in his own bed, so he bailed from the party to take a nap. Anne diligently helped him out of his chair and onto his bed. "Did you want to change?"

"No, I'm fine to sleep in sweatpants. I'm exhausted."

"I bet you are." Anne brushed his cheek with the back of her hand. "I love you. I have my phone with me. Text me if you need me for anything."

"What's this?" Peter pointed to a manila envelope on his pillow.

"Olivia gave me that last time we met for coffee. She said to give it to you after you got better."

Peter furrowed his eyebrows. "What is it?"

Anne shrugged her shoulders. "I think it's from Gwen."

He looked awkwardly at the envelope. Anne said, "I'll give you some privacy." As she back out of the door she said, "I love you." Then she disappeared.

Peter clutched the envelope, noting the outside was unmarked. He ripped the corner of the envelope and tore it open along the seam. Peering inside, he saw a CD case. He grabbed it and recognized it immediately as his recording he made with Ambrose of their song *"Should've Asked You First." This is the CD I had burned for my mom.* He opened the case and a folded piece of paper fell out.

Picking up the paper, he unfolded it and right away recognized Gwen's handwriting.

Pete—I just got done listening to your song. Your mom sent this to my mom, and my mom gave it to me. I wish so much that I could call you, but I feel like such a coward. The truth is Brad checks my phone, and he doesn't like me talking to you. I guess that's why I'm writing this letter. I just needed to tell you in some way that I know the song you wrote was for me, and I loved it. Maybe I didn't see it before, and maybe that's why I don't deserve you, but I think about how things could have been different a lot. I miss you.

Your forever friend, Gwen

Peter read the letter, then released it, allowing it to fall onto his bedspread. He closed his eyes to picture her face, but his thoughts were interrupted by the doorbell ringing. He paused listening for footsteps passing his room to answer the door, but the house seemed empty. Pounding sounded from the front door and the doorbell rang again. "Can someone get the door?" Peter yelled. The house was quiet. Peter scooted as far as he could to the edge of his bed and placed one hand on his wheelchair to brace himself. He pushed himself up and then pivoted his feet on the ground until he was centered in front of his chair enough so he could sit back.

The doorbell rang again. "I'm coming! Hold on!" he yelled. *Good grief, where is everyone?* Peter wheeled himself through the house and looked for his family. He found them outside through the kitchen window. It looked like they were playing some sort of lawn game, maybe beanbags. When he reached the foyer and opened the door, he found two men in uniforms standing on the step. "Are you Peter Arnold?" one of the men asked.

"Yeah."

"I'm Detective Stanford. He held up a badge. I'm wondering if we could have a little chat." Peter looked from the badge to the officer. He robotically opened the door further to allow the man inside. The first man went in, but the second man stood still. "I'm Officer Everhardt." He held up his badge too.

"Hi, can I help you?"

"We are hoping you can." He smiled and then followed the first officer inside.

AN HOUR LATER, PETER SAT ACROSS FROM DETECTIVE SANFORD AT THE police station, ready for what the police had called a 'helpful interview.' Two other officers stood against the wall.

"Thanks for coming down, Peter," the detective said. "We appreciate you helping us out."

"You're welcome. Not sure how much help I can be, but I'll do my best."

"Like I said, we are investigating the accident that killed Ambrose Black. I hear you just got back from France. You were staying with him as a roommate?" Detective Sanford asked.

"Yeah," Peter said, hoping he could help the officer out.

"That must have been a nice place to stay. Did he charge you rent?"

"I didn't pay rent." Peter shook his head. "We had a different arrangement."

"Really, like what?" The officer raised an inquiring brow.

Peter thought for a minute, realizing how weird everything was going to sound, but he didn't have anything to hide so he said, "Ambrose told me I had to live there to record a song with him."

A confused look set on the officer's face. "Why would he require you to live with him?"

"I thought he was trying to get to know me."

"Why would he want to do that?"

"Well, because I'm his biological son."

"Really." The officer looked over at one of the other officers who was standing behind him. They exchanged a look before asking another question. "So what were you recording?"

"We recorded a song together."

"So, like a song that you were going to release?"

"I thought that was the plan." Peter explained as he leaned back further into his chair, realizing this interview was going to take longer than he had thought. "Ambrose never followed through with getting the studio artists to record their parts, and so we never gave it to either of our labels."

"That's too bad. Do you know why?"

Peter sighed, as it wasn't really hard for him to think about everything that he had been through with Ambrose, but he didn't like talking about him, knowing he had passed. "He told me he wanted to keep it private until after I died, so it would be worth more money."

"That's terrible." The officer offered a disapproving frown. "Did he think you were dying?"

"Well yeah, I told him I was dying because I was."

"But you're not dead."

"No, I had a kidney transplant."

"You received Ambrose's kidney, right?"

"Yes." Peter started to feel a little uneasy about how all these details sounded as he stated them out loud.

"Did Ambrose arrange for you to have his kidney?"

"Well, yeah or no. He said, well, he never promised it to me, but he made me believe he would give it to me if I helped him."

"So, did you help him?" The officer leaned forward, in an inquiring manner.

"I did what he asked."

"Then he offered you the kidney?"

"Not exactly. He said I would never get it."

The officer was silent, tapping his fingers on the table in front of him before changing the subject. "You know, Ambrose was alive when he arrived at the hospital. He told the nurses there some stuff."

"Oh," Peter said.

"He said he was pushed out the window."

Instantly confused, Peter felt his brows pull together but he was quiet because he didn't like the expression the officer had on his face.

"Were you in the tower with him that day?"

"Yes," Peter squeaked out, feeling like this friendly conversation was taking a whole different turn.

"Was there anyone else there?"

"Just me, and then my mom and Doc helped me, but they left when I did."

"Did you have a nice conversation?"

"No, we fought," Peter's voice cracked.

"What did you fight about?"

"Uh, the song we recorded and the fact he wasn't going to give me a kidney."

The officer tilted his head slightly and confirmed, "You knew that day he wasn't going to give you a kidney?"

"That's what he said."

"So then how come you showed up at the hospital a couple hours later to ask for his kidney?"

Peter's mouth was drained from all moisture, making words stick to the back of this throat. After a moment of failed attempts to speak, he asked, "Can I have some water?"

One of the officers standing against the door left the room to get Peter a cup of water, came back, and set it in front of Peter. He took a sip and after he had set the cup back down the officer in front of him leaned forward again and pressed, "Peter, how did you know to come to the hospital?"

"Doc called me. He said there was an accident."

"What did you think when you heard that?"

"I didn't think much." Peter still struggled to speak, now feeling his brow starting to dampen, but he plowed through the pressure and said, "I mean, he was drunk when I left him. I assumed he had lost his balance."

"It's tragic." The officer said, his voice filled with empathy. Then he let his eyes dig into Peter's and he waited, saying nothing. Peter chewed the side of his cheek, now knowing that there was absolutely something wrong with this conversation.

After way too long of a silence, the officer said, "Also, I was looking at your plans for that day, and you had put your name on a standby fly list."

"Yeah, my mom did that."

"You were trying to leave the country. Why such a hurry?"

"It was just time."

"Hmm." He narrowed his eyes and continued to stare at Peter.

"Look, Detective, I'm happy to help you with what I know, but you don't think I had anything to do with his death, do you?"

"We don't think that. We just wanted to know if you could tell us more about the accident."

"I don't know anything. I wasn't there. I had already left."

"Tell me about your music again. The one you recorded with Ambrose. What were you guys planning to do with it?"

"I didn't have a plan," Peter blurted out, now feeling exhausted from all the questions. "I didn't even want to record it."

"Two big celebrities record a song together. Wouldn't you want to sell it to make money?"

"No, that was *his* plan. I don't even have access to the song. The demo is in his studio. I couldn't care less about it."

The detective reached into a bag and pulled out a sealed plastic bag and laid it on the table. Inside the bag was something Peter recognized. His heart sank. "I found a CD recording lying on your bed. It matches the description of the song Ambrose told the nurse that you had stolen from him."

Peter's mouth dropped open. "I gave that CD to my mom, and she sent it to a friend and that friend's mom gave it back to me. It's not even the final recording. It was just a first recording for my mom. I literally just found it again before you guys showed up at my house."

"Is that the same song on the CD?"

"Well, yeah, but I forgot about that copy."

"Yeah, that happens. Don't worry about it. No big deal. We wanted to make sure we were all on the same page here." He smiled one of those smiles like you would see coming from Mr. Grinch. "So, it worked out that you got the kidney you needed. That's really something. I'm happy for you."

"Um, thanks."

"Did your operation go well?"

"Yeah."

"Was it pretty expensive to have a transplant?"

"I have insurance, but you know it never covers everything, that's for sure."

"Do you have unpaid medical bills?"

Peter wasn't dumb, he knew these guys knew he had money and he wasn't ever comfortable talking about his finances, so he stated, "I'm fortunate I had money to pay them."

"But was it enough?"

"So far."

"You never asked Ambrose for any money?"

"No, I have my own. I don't need his."

"Peter, there's something else that turns out to be good news for you."

"What?" Peter asked, feeling like this good news was actually going to be really bad news.

"Ambrose's lawyer is the administrator of his trust and will."

"Okay," he said.

"Ambrose was pretty wealthy. Did you know that?"

"I guess." Peter shrugged, ready to be done with this conversation. "He's famous. I know what I make. I can imagine what he's made over the years."

Detective Sanford looked down at the file and read from a list. "His estate includes three executive homes in Europe, a handful of luxury vehicles, a couple million in fine art. With stocks and cash reserves, it all totals over 150 million dollars."

"Okay," Peter said, feeling unimpressed.

The officer locked eyes with Peter again, paused for a brief moment and then said, "In his will, he left it all to you."

Peter jerked his head back as if he didn't hear correctly. "Huh?"

"You heard me. I know you said you don't need his money, but you are about to be an even more wealthy man. How great is that?"

"I just, I think that's a mistake. He would never leave me a dime," Peter managed to mutter from his state of confusion. The detective slipped a sheet of paper across the table. It was Ambrose's will, and Peter's name was listed as the beneficiary. Detective Sanford slid his finger down to the bottom where Ambrose had signed it. He held his finger by the date. It had been updated a week before his death.

Peter's eyes shifted from the paper to the detective. He had a knot in his stomach and he didn't like that stupid grin on the officer's face. "I think I need to call my lawyer."

CHAPTER TWENTY-THREE

*B*ack at home the next day, it was obvious to Peter his room had been rummaged through. He resented that an outsider could go through his personal space. His mom pushed the door opened slightly. "Can I come in?"

"I guess."

"I know you don't want to talk about this, and I know you didn't have anything to do with it, but I wanted to tell you that I had an officer come over to chat with me after you left yesterday."

Flashing an annoyed look at her, Peter asked, "Really?"

"I think they needed to get my testimony on file."

"This is the most absurd thing." Peter ran a hand through his hair. With everything that had happened in the last few months, he hadn't had time for a haircut, and his hair had grown to his shoulders.

"I can only think they're doing it to make their job easy. I mean, who are they going to blame?"

Peter glared at his mom.

"You think Doc did it?" Anne asked.

"No, I don't. But he was the only one who was left alone with Ambrose so why wouldn't they suspect him?"

"I'm sure they questioned him, too. But maybe it was ruled out because he's innocent, like we all are."

"I don't know. He did tell me he wanted to steal Ambrose's kidney while he was sleeping."

"I'm sure he didn't mean it. He was frustrated like we all were."

"I don't know."

Anne let out a giggle.

Peter scowled at Anne. "Why are you laughing?"

Anne tried to suppress it, but couldn't. It made Peter chuckle a little. "What are you laughing about?"

"I'm not laughing about this cause it's not funny. I think it's ironic how everything we've been through and now we have this. But you know, you'll be okay. They'll never have any evidence against you because you didn't do it."

"I don't know how they do crime research overseas, but I'm nervous because I don't have the best of luck with life—if you haven't figured it out already."

"It'll be okay. I have a feeling about this one. I mean honestly, you can ask your transplant doctors—who can testify that you would never have even been physically capable of pushing anyone—especially a grown man. You were so frail back then."

Thomas appeared in the doorway. "Hi," he said, looking forlorn and exhausted.

"Hi," Anne said. "What are you doing home from work?"

Thomas walked into the now crowded tiny bedroom, shutting the door to shield Peter's siblings from the conversation. "I have to go back to the office, but I wanted to check in to make sure you guys were okay."

Peter said, "Good as I can be."

"Are those reporters outside bothering you guys at all? They were in my face when I tried to walk past," Thomas said.

"They're terrible," Anne commented. "There was only one here this morning when I left the house, but ever since then there have been at least two or three all day."

"Dad! Peter!" Shiloh's voice called from the living room. Thomas opened the door and yelled out. "What?"

"Can you come out here? Peter's lawyer is here."

"Now what?" Anne asked.

Peter sighed. "Welcome to my life." He rolled his wheelchair through the door.

James Birdee Jr. stood in the doorway, looking more like an ex-con than he did a lawyer. He was a professional body builder in his spare time and he was also part owner of the local tattoo shop, so he had his share of body art. "Hey, I have good news for you!"

Peter braced himself for whatever news was going to be thrown at him. "How about you tell me what it is; I'll decide whether it's good news."

"Another witness has popped up as to being there when Ambrose fell, and after questioning, they are detaining that person as their main suspect and are making plans to have them taken back to France for investigations. Which means, they no longer need any help from you at this time."

"Thank God," Peter said.

Anne sighed loudly. "That is good news. But who else was there?"

James spoke, "It's all private information for now."

"That's the best news ever," Peter said, feeling a strange chill come over him as he realized there was more to the accident than he had known.

"I have to caution you," James went on, "this is not over. Please, don't speak about this to anyone or do anything that looks suspicious. Until the person is convicted, you never know how these investigations go, but as of now they have no grounds to suspect you or even question you."

"Well, can you tell me one thing?" Peter asked.

"What?" James replied.

"Was it Doc?"

James shook his head. "I doubt it. According to what I know, he was cleared right away. He was never even a suspect."

Peter looked to Anne, who stared back with an equally puzzled look. "But who else was there?" Peter asked.

CHAPTER TWENTY-FOUR

*W*eeks went by, and Peter heard nothing more about the investigation, but he tried to keep a low profile anyway. Aside from his transplant checkups, he also started physical therapy again, and most mornings he had a private driver take him to the coffee shop after those appointments, but other than that, he stayed home.

"Peter! Come quick," Thomas's voice boomed from the living room. When Peter got to the living room, his parents and Shiloh stared at the TV. It was one of those ridiculous celebrity gossip news reports.

"Why do you guys watch that garbage?" Peter asked.

"We weren't. I accidentally clicked on this channel; but look," Thomas said. Peter turned his attention to the reporter who was talking about Ambrose's death and they had uncovered the name of the person who was now the suspected murderer—it was Exa!

Peter wheeled his chair right up in front of the TV. The reporter went through details about how Exa's passport had proved she had been in France that day, and they even had witnesses claiming that she stayed at a hotel close to Ambrose's castle. The program ended and a commercial about dishwashing soap flashed across the screen. Peter turned his head toward his parents. "I don't believe it."

"Have you talked to her lately?" Thomas asked.

Peter exhaled, deeply. "I remember calling her when I was in France, and we talked a little. She told me to leave and get away from Ambrose before he hurt me."

Anne's eyebrows furrowed. "So she knew he had lied to you?"

Peter shrugged, starting to feel a little guilt for involving her in his issues. "I don't remember a lot from back then because I wasn't feeling the best, but I can't imagine she would do that."

"What would be her motive?" Thomas asked.

Peter's mind raced, but it was who Anne spoke, "Well, you know how these shows are. They tend to elaborate to sell to an audience. Maybe it's nothing." The tone in her voice wasn't as convincing as she wanted it to be and Peter was let thinking, *Exa always has been a dark horse, but was she capable of murder?*

CHAPTER TWENTY-FIVE

*a*fter a sleepless night, Peter was notified by James of the news confirming Exa was going to be charged with one count of first degree murder. In his heart, he had been blown a bullet.

Rain pitter-pattered on Peter's window while he stared down at the garage that used to be his studio. Now, it housed the sports car he was no longer able to drive. Chewing his lip, he came up with a plan, then texted Paul.

"Hey, Paul."

"Hey."

"What are you doing?"

"Getting ready to make the deposit for the coffee shop. Why?"

"I was thinking about something. Thanks for taking care of the shop for me."

"You're welcome."

"I want to give you my car."

"Ha ha."

"No, I'm not joking. I can't drive it. I can sell it, but I thought it might be more fun for you to have it. She's a rush to drive."

"If you insist."

"I do."

"Thanks, Peter."

"You're welcome. Thanks for your help. I'll drop the keys off sometime."

Peter sent his last text message, remembering how he had once told Gwen she could have his car after he died. He would have never imagined in a million years that she would have gone off and married some loser who made her cut him out of her life. Things just never turned out the way he would have thought.

He took a cab to the coffee shop later that night on his way back from physical therapy. He was tired, but didn't feel like going home yet. The coffee shop was closed and empty—exactly what he needed. Smiling to himself, he placed his car keys in the tip jar for Paul to find them in the morning. Then he got to work, burning four shots of espresso before he got one to come out skinny like a mouse's tail, like it was supposed to look. He poured water on top of his perfect single shot of espresso and closed the lid on the cup with the Gwen's Daily Grind label on it.

Retreating to his usual spot by the door, he put his feet on the coffee table and leaned his head back, closing his eyes. He must've fallen asleep, because in what felt like moments later, he was awoken by the sound of the doorknob jiggling. Thinking it must have been Paul coming back to do something, he watched the door open, but to his surprise, Gwen walked through the door.

"Hi." She held her petite hand up in a light wave while she stepped through the door.

"Hi." Peter startled in his seat, and hurried to sit up straight, running a hand through his hair, hoping he didn't look like a total bum because he hadn't even showered that morning.

"Your mom said she thought you'd be here. I hope you don't mind but I still had a key. Can I come in?"

Not believing his eyes, he stammered, "Uh, sure."

She closed the door behind her, and took another step closer to Peter, and asked, "How are you?"

"Uh, Fine."

"Here, take your key before I forget I have it again." She carefully removed a key from her key chain and slid it on the table next to Peter. Then she motioned to the chair next to his. "Can I sit here?"

"Sure." He shot a look back to the door, expecting to see Brad. "You by yourself?"

"Yeah." She sat, removing her coat.

"Brad let you come here?"

She sighed heavily. "He doesn't know I'm here." Then she lowered her eyes and said, "I haven't talked to him in months."

"Oh . . ." His brows pulled up with his interest fully peaked.

"Maybe you didn't know; I called off the wedding the night before."

"Really?" Still amazed that he was looking at Gwen sitting next to him, he was completely confused to what was happening and at a loss for words.

"I don't think I need to tell you that you were right about him," she said. "I was rushing into it, and when I took the time to slow down and think, I started to see how he was controlling me." She let her eyes raise to meet his, and for the first time in a long time, he noticed the sadness they had held was gone.

"Can you say that again?"

"Say what?" The corners of Gwen's mouth pulled up slightly when she sensed Peter was teasing.

"That part about how I was right."

"You were." Resting her eyes on her hands that were folded in her lap, she continued, "You were completely right, and I thank you for pointing that out to me when no one else would."

Peter could feel an easing of his breath as he saw in Gwen her old self and he became completely at ease with her. "Sorry I was right. You okay?"

"I'm learning to be." Then she raised her face again and asked "So, how are you?"

"You already asked me that. Fine."

"Good." She stared at him, giving him that look they always shared, and Peter began to believe she was really returning back to be true to herself.

Feeling intrigued, he asked, "So, tell me, what have you been up to?"

"A lot actually," she started in a relieved tone. "After Brad left, I decided to give it one more shot and do the chemo again. I realized it was his controlling behavior that had pressured me not to do it. So of course I wanted to prove to him I could do it. It was terrible. *Chemo didn't work.*"

"What?" Peter leaned forward, feeling a new fear of losing her creep in.

"It's okay." She raised her hand in an assuring way. "We did the bone marrow transplant thing after that. I got super sick, and I wanted to die, but to my surprise it looks like it worked for now."

Peter sat up even straighter in his chair, now understanding how serious Gwen's illness had really been and feeling relieved for her. "That's awesome. Do you feel healthy?"

"Yeah, I do. I get tired, but I can also tell I'm getting stronger every day."

"That's amazing. I'm so happy for you." Peter's expression lifted. "It's the best news ever."

"It is. It's unbelievable and I find myself being hopeful again."

"I knew you could beat it. I'm glad you changed your mind. You have so much life to live."

"I wanted to tell you because you were a big part of why I decided to give it another try." Her words were slow and well thought out. "You never gave up, and when I heard you had a successful surgery, I knew I could try too."

Peter inclined his chin toward her. "So are you saying I was right again?"

"Stop it." Gwen grinned broadly. "I can see your ego inflating by the minute."

Peter laughed. "So you just happen to be in town, or . . .?"

"No, I came here to see you. I gave my mom a package to give to your mom. Did you get it?"

"I did." Peter felt himself freeze, feeling exposed, remembering all the emotion he had poured into that song. He had never intended Gwen to ever hear it. Now it was awkward to have to look at her, because she knew everything he had been feeling.

"I sort of thought that maybe you would have called me."

"Actually"—Peter let his head tilt to the side—"I sort of got arrested. Well, not arrested, but the police had me come down for questioning for a murder and that package was used against me as evidence."

Gwen quickly slid her hand over her mouth. "You're joking."

Peter gave her his dead-serious expression. "No, I'm not."

"I heard there was some drama about Ambrose's death. Didn't Exa have something to do with it?"

"Evidently she confessed. But for a few days, it didn't look good for me, and the CD that you sent me was sort of the evidence to make me look like a liar."

"I didn't know." She tried to conceal her amusement but ended up letting a quiet giggle release through her sealed lips. "Here, I thought you were ignoring me, but you were, in fact, breaking the law."

"You know me. I'm a trouble maker."

"Sorry."

"I guess I'll forgive you and on the bright side I got to mark being a suspect for murder off my bucket list."

"That's good to do. So maybe I was right about Exa?"

Peter looked down thoughtfully at his cup, not wanting to get into it. He shrugged his shoulders and said, "I'm sure there's more there than what people know."

"It's just like you to defend her."

Peter quickly shot his eyes back at her, and warned, "Don't start."

"No, I'm not. Sorry. I wasn't trying to be snotty. I think it's great how loyal you are to her."

"You mean that?"

Gwen nodded slightly. "I do." Her eyes smiled at him, sparkling more than he had ever seen them do.

"You seem like you've changed, haven't you?"

"Maybe. I do feel a lot more optimistic about things now that my life is on a new path. It's a little embarrassing when I think about how far I fell, but I guess maybe I'm stronger because of it."

"I would be embarrassed about Brad too."

"Stop it." Gwen playfully pushed Peter's shoulder. "Anyway, you look like you're doing well. You have some color in your face. Last time I saw you, you were pretty pale."

Peter scratched the back of his head, not sure of what to think of this conversation. "Do you want something to drink? I'd offer to make you something, but my lack of barista skills would prolly accidentally poison you with some lingering listeria bugs or something, but you're welcome to help yourself."

"The mouthwash?"

"Not Listerine, listeria. It's the most common pathogen that lives in dairy products."

"I prolly missed that day of school."

"It's okay." His lips slid easily over his teeth into a wide grin. He just felt so amazing, sitting here next to her. "No one's grading anymore."

Gwen looked sideways at Peter and there was a new gleam in her eyes when she asked, "Do you know what I want?"

"Didn't you always like those London Fog teas?"

She licked her lips lightly then said, "I wasn't talking about coffee."

"What were you talking about?"

"I want to go back to that day in France at the airport."

Peter couldn't understand why but he could feel his heart starting to thumb hard against his rib cage and he couldn't stop looking at her. "Oh . . ."

She went on, "I've have replayed that day in my head so many times. I'm sorry. I never meant to be mean to you. I hate how I acted."

"It's okay," Peter said in a voice so soft it was barely audible. "I was probably out of line."

"Why do you say that?"

He raised a shoulder, and offered, "I did say stuff about Brad."

"You were right about Brad."

"You can say that as many times as you want."

Gwen giggled, and Peter could hear a weird hint of nervousness in it, that confused him, but then she continued, "It took me a while to hear it, but I did eventually listen to you. I know you were looking out for me."

"He didn't deserve you." Peter looked down at his hand holding his coffee. "So, are you staying with your mom?"

Gwen smiled shyly. "Are you changing the subject on purpose?"

"Maybe." Peter smiled back.

"Does that conversation make you nervous?"

"I don't like talking about Brad. You know that."

"But what about the other thing we talked about at the airport?"

Peter felt his heart drop what felt like an inch.

"I was super scared of that conversation then, so I ran away, and I sort of regretted it ever since," Gwen blurted out.

"It's okay. I prolly would have run away from me too."

"Sorry for being dumb and putting you through all my drama. I hope we can be friends still."

The knot of inferiority that was frequently in his stomach when he thought of only being Gwen's *friend* returned. "Of course," he said, looking down at his coffee cup again. "You wanna turn the radio on?"

She pressed another smile on her lips. "You're changing the subject again."

"I didn't. We were done talking about it, weren't we?"

She took the coffee cup out of his hand and set it on the table. Grabbing both of his hands. "I'm not done talking about it, but it still really scares me, so I don't know how to continue."

His cheeks warmed. "I'm sort of confused," he started to say slowly, and then continued even slower, "I think, I know what you're referring to, but I've been really wrong before, so I might need you to be a *little* more specific."

The smile that spread on her lips made tiny goosebumps trace up his arms. It was genuine, beautiful, and held a flirtation he had never seen before. Leaning toward him just a slight measure further, she whispered, "I think you were right about that other thing too."

"I do love hearing you say that I was right." His voice cracked a note higher from the tightening of his airway. He stopped to take a full breath, and when he felt able, he asked, "Which thing are you referring too?"

"I hope I'm not too late," she hesitated, holding her eyes in communion with his, and letting her bottom lip roll under her teeth. Then she added, "But, I think you were right about us being perfect for each other."

He held his breath and looked down at their hands entangled together. He always hated the way his hands looked all knotted at the joints, but when her fingers threaded through his, her hands covered the ugliness that embarrassed him. In that moment, he knew exactly what she had meant when she said that when you love someone, you want to do anything you can to make them happy, because all he wanted to do was make her happy—forever.

He squeezed her hands, thinking of a way to tease her about being right again, but it didn't matter anymore. He didn't need to be funny, or right. Looking deeply into her eyes, he said, "I think so too."

CHAPTER TWENTY-SIX

"*W*here are you taking me?" Gwen waddled forward with her pregnant belly, seven-months huge. "Are we going back to Ambrose's house?" Earlier that day, Peter had surprised his wife, with a trip to France, and they had been up for hours, traveling but both were too excited to stop to rest.

Because of Gwen's high-risk pregnancy, Peter convinced Thomas to tag along. Thomas had been reluctant to intrude but understood how it would ease their stress, and he mostly tried to stay in the background and go unnoticed. "I had no idea I would ever get to go on my son's honeymoon," Thomas teased as he pulled luggage from the cab trunk.

"We had a honeymoon. This is just a trip for fun. Sort of a babymoon," Peter said. "Stop here," he told them and removed the bandana from Gwen's face.

Her face froze as she stared at the house in front of her. She didn't recognize it and she immediately asked, "Where are we?"

"Technically at our house."

She gazed at the charming French chateau in Loire Valley, looming before her. "What are you talking about?"

"I told you before I had inherited Ambrose's estate. He had several properties in France. This was one of the ones I haven't had time to visit yet and I thought it would be fun to spend the week here."

Her smile spread so wide across her face, it instantly warmed Peter's heart to see her so happy by his surprise. "I can't wait to see it," she exclaimed.

Peter knocked on the front door. Gwen furrowed her eyebrows. "Why are you knocking?" Before he could answer, the door swung opened, and Doc greeted them with a grin.

"Doc! What are you doing here?" Gwen squealed, excitedly as she leaned in to hug him.

"I didn't tell her," Peter explained to Doc.

"That was sneaky of you."

"It was a surprise," Peter defended.

Doc leaned back to look at Gwen. "You look amazing. Absolutely glowing. How do you feel?"

"Like a Butterball turkey on Thanksgiving morning, ready to pop out my little meter thingy that says I'm done cooking."

Doc chuckled loudly. "Come inside. And it's so nice to meet you finally, Mr. Arnold."

"Call me Thomas." Thomas said, reaching over to shake Doc's hand.

"I will. Welcome to France." He waved them all inside the house, and said, "I finished making a salad for dinner tonight, and it's chilling in the fridge. I should have the rest done in an hour. So I'll give you a tour and show you where your rooms are located."

"So why are you here?" Gwen asked Doc.

"I asked him to come," Peter explained. This house has been sitting empty for years. I had no idea what the condition was, so I asked him to come get it ready for us."

"It actually wasn't too bad. It needed a deep cleaning, but everything was preserved well." Doc explained while he walked through the foyer. "There's the kitchen and dining in that direction. This house has an atrium which is fascinating, and I would love to get it functioning. It's right past the music room over here."

"I can't believe you owned his house and never told me. It's gorgeous." Gwen looked at Peter in amazement.

"I honestly never thought about it much. This last year has been a blur. And technically—he beamed at her—it's our home."

"It's a grand house, too," Doc agreed. "I'm interviewing full-time care-takers tomorrow. I got a few with great references. I'm hoping to have them trained in by the end of the month, so I can get back to tending your other house."

"Thank you for all you do, Doc," Peter said. "I know it's a lot. Let me know if you need more help."

"Nah, I enjoy it. It definitely keeps me out of trouble."

"Trouble? What kind of trouble would you get into?" Gwen teased.

Doc's cheeks pinked. "I feel foolish at my age to even say it out loud, but I met someone."

"What?" That's amazing!" Gwen said.

"I had no idea," Peter said. "Who is she?"

"I've known her for years. She runs the bakery down the street from the house."

"That's too funny. Of course, she runs the bakery. Do you mean Hannah?" Peter asked.

"That's the one." Doc grinned, like a young lad who was experiencing puppy love for the first time. "She's been widowed for ten years, and we always had a similar affection for great pastries. I guess it grew into an affection for each other."

"I'm happy for you," Gwen said. "I can't wait to meet her."

"I'm happy for me too," Doc said as he turned by the music room. "Here is the back-staircase. I'm staying up there right in the first room, so not too far if you need help. There's a room a little further down the hall that I thought would be perfect for you, Thomas. It has a lovely view."

"I'm sure it will be great," Thomas said.

"If you just head up these stairs and go to the second door, you will find it."

"Okay, thanks. I'll get my stuff put away and come down when I am settled." Thomas left up the stairs.

"I set up your room over here." Doc turned on his heel to open a door across the hall from the staircase. "This was the original mother-in-law suite, but it works perfectly for you because there are no stairs. You two go ahead; I will go grab your luggage and bring it in. I'll also have tea ready in the sitting room whenever you're ready. And Hannah sent some of her French butter cookies for us."

"Thanks, Doc," Gwen said, entering the room.

"Yeah, thanks. It's really great being here with you again," Peter said as he lingered by the door next to Doc.

Doc's face showed nothing but contentment when he said, "I'm very glad to see you again too." Then after a quiet exchange of appreciative looks, Doc left, leaving the couple alone.

AFTER A BEAUTIFUL DINNER AND FAMILY TIME, PETER SAT UP IN BED, reading travel blogs on his phone. Gwen quietly pushed the door opened and not so gracefully bumped the table next to the door, causing a lamp to wobble. "Oh bother." She reached forward to steady it from falling. "I can't see where my body begins anymore." She giggled. "I can't imagine how much bigger I'm going to get." She waddled over to the edge of the bed, grabbing a hairbrush from her bag.

Peter watched her brush her hair back. "You look beautiful."

Then replacing her brush into her bag, she pulled out a couple of round pieces of chocolate, unwrapping one and popping it into her mouth.

"What are those?"

"Baby needs peanut butter cups," she said through a mouthful of food.

"I think Mom needs peanut butter cups," Peter teased, letting a laugh escape his lips.

She shook her head innocently. "No, I don't care for them. I'm eating these strictly because baby wanted them. Gotta take care of baby. It's like child neglect if I didn't."

"Oh yeah, totally the same thing."

Looking around the room, Gwen inhaled deeply and then said, "Thanks for bringing me here. I can't wait to explore in the morning."

"We can do whatever you want. I have nothing planned."

She winced, and leaned forward, grabbing her heart.

Peter raised a concern brow. "You feeling okay?"

"I think so." She breathed a slow breath. "It's those heart palpitations. I probably need to take some more magnesium."

"Are you sure that's all?" His eyes darted to the door. "I can get my dad."

"No. I'm fine." She put a reassuring hand on his arm. "Just completely worn out and ready to rest." She lifted the covers and slid over next to him to snuggle. However, it was only another short moment before she held her heart again. "I can't believe how strong they are. Can I have some of your water?"

He promptly retrieved his water bottle from his nightstand and said, "Here, you keep it."

"Thanks." She took a sip, and set it next to her. "I don't know if it was the flight or the baby or what, but I could prolly lie in bed all week and have the best vacation ever."

"Nothing wrong with spending a week in bed."

Gwen grinned at him, but Peter noticed she did look exhausted. Now worried, he asked, "Are you sure you're okay?"

"I'm fine. I honestly feel like the luckiest girl in the world right now. The most tired, but the luckiest."

"Then rest." He kissed her softly on the lips. Then she rolled over, pulling the blanket up closer, tucking it under her chin.

"Night, honey. Love you," she said with her eyes already closed.

"Love you too."

"GWEN! WHERE ARE YOU?" IN A DREAM THAT NIGHT, PETER ROUNDED A broken stone path in the cemetery, barely keeping his balance on the uneven cobble stones. "Gwen!"

"Marco," her voice called from the distance.

"Gwen, I don't want to play your games. Where are you?" He looked around paranoid, creeped out by the tombstones.

"Marco." The voice faded.

He sighed, giving into her game and said, "Polo."

"Marco." Her voice came out in echoes. It seemed to come from all around him.

"Polo." Walking forward, he looked through the pine trees for her. He tripped, falling to his knees, but then he saw lilies—purple lilies everywhere and they appeared to be covering a fresh gravesite.

"You okay?" She appeared, reaching her hand down to help him up. "Where's your wheelchair?"

"I'm trying to be tough like you told me to be." He stood back up, looking at her. She looked radiant in a long, white sundress with her blond curls hanging loose down her back. "Why are we here?" he asked.

"I guess for old times' sake. Remember when we used to play hide-and-seek here?"

"I do. We did a lot of stupid stuff together."

"What's wrong? You look distraught?" Gwen asked.

"Something feels weird."

Her lips bent down, and her face instantly saddened. "You don't know?"

"Know what?"

Gwen reached out, taking his hand. He felt it envelop his hand like a glove, but there was a warmth missing. She touched his cheek with her free hand. Peter felt her physically touch him, but there was a tenderness that was gone. "Peter, I'm crossing over."

He waited for her to elaborate, but she didn't. Instead, she turned to the nearest tombstone—the one covered in purple lilies—and bent down near it. Pulling a few lilies away, she revealed the headstone: Gweneveire Arnold June 21, 1997—May 10, 2016.

"That's today's date," Peter said, feeling confused. Looking around him, and then back to Gwen. He stuttered out, "But, you're here?"

"This is just a dream." She looked at him, her eyes filled with agony. "However, it's really me speaking. My time is up. I've been allowed the special privilege to say goodbye to you, but I can't take any extra time, but there's something else, and I'm afraid it's dire."

Peter's chest filled with despair, and he reached for her, but his hand seemed to go right through her. "What are you talking about?" He cried out.

Her eyes moved to the side and he followed them to a tree a few yards away. A beautiful apple tree blossomed with white flowers. It had a low branch that stuck out horizontally holding a homemade swing. A simple wood board with two ropes swung back and forth in the wind. As he watched the board swing, a figure materialized. It was a girl, about the age of three. She was wearing a white sundress like Gwen's, and a huge smile that playfully giggled. Golden pigtails bounced from her head as she pumped her legs to go higher.

He heard Gwen catch her breath in a gasp as she watched the girl. "It's her."

"Who?"

"It's our daughter," she whispered, her voice filled with a loving awe. "She's in-between too. She's not supposed to be here. I was told she was going to live."

"This is scary," Peter said, looking around paranoid, tears welling in his eyes. "I want to wake up—"

"—I don't have much time," Gwen interrupted, "so I have to say good-bye." Her eyes were tearfully focused on the little girl.

"No!"

"It's too late for me." She looked back at Peter. "My heart can't do it anymore."

"What are you saying? How? You were fine."

"I'm sorry, but I have to move on."

Peter reached for her again and this time he was able to hold her, and he pulled her into his arms. His heart plummeted when he felt her body was cold. In a panic, he cried, "I can't let go!"

"I wish things were different, but I can't stay." She flashed a look at him, but then turned back to the girl. "It's the most beautiful face I've ever seen."

"She looks just like you," Peter said, and it was now his turn to whisper as his words were getting so hard to express.

"I could just look at that face forever."

Peter turned back to Gwen and said, "I always thought the same thing about you."

Gwen swallowed hard, and then said, "You know, I won't even get to hold her."

"I'm sorry." Peter's lip quivered. "I don't understand what is happening." His hands slipped from her body. He reached forward to pull her near again, but his hand went right through her this time. She was turning into a blue shadow, fading in and out.

Then she was gone but he heard her voice, "Peter, I love you. But you have to wake up and help our daughter or she won't make it. There's no time. Wake up!" Her voice was cutting in and out. "Wake up now!"

"I don't want to leave you!" He called out into the empty cemetery.

"Her name is—" and then in a moment so fast he didn't have time to protest, he woke up, sat up straight and said the word, "Lily."

He let his eyes adjust to the darkness then realized he had just had the cruelest of nightmares. His sheet was soaked from a cold body sweat. Peeling it back off him, he leaned over to snuggle Gwen. His new relief was quickly stolen when he rested his face next to hers because he felt an odd dampness on her pillow. Confused, he brushed his fingers over it, noticing it was a runny discharge that appeared to come from her nose. "Gwen," he said softly, but there was no movement from her. Panic set in and he felt her forehead with the back of his hand. It was still a little warm, but he could tell something was wrong. She wasn't moving with her breath. "Gwen!" He tried to lift her face to his to feel her breath. "*Oh God, please* no!" he begged.

"Dad!" He screamed at the top of his lungs. "Dad, I need you fast!" He leaned over her, and sobbed. "Wake up, Gwen. Don't let this be real."

CHAPTER TWENTY-SEVEN

FIVE YEARS LATER

*P*eter wheeled his chair through the front door of the coffee shop and was immediately met with a fresh-faced, smiling Exa, who to Peter's surprise was wearing a bright yellow dress. She leaned in, hugging him tightly. "Pe ta, I've missed you."

Not able to take his eyes off the color of her dress, Peter had never remembered her wearing any other color other than black in all the years he had known her. "You look great," he stuttered.

"Thank you." She received his complement with a loving smile.

Motioning to the counter, he offered, "Can I get you a coffee?"

"I got one already." She pointed to her cup, sitting on the table, already half empty. "I came early. I couldn't wait to do something normal like sit in a coffee shop."

"I bet. Well, sit back down. I can't wait to hear how everything is going." He waved a hand over to his part-time gal who was working.

She smiled and asked, "Decaf Americano?"

"Please," he said, and sat, focusing back on Exa, who was eager to visit.

Looking relieved, she took another drink of her coffee. Then in a smooth voice, filled with contentment, she said, "It feels like a rebirth to be out in the world again."

Peter was still so confused by the recent news, he had to ask, "So what happened? How did you get your sentence reduced so much?"

"Long story. It's good behavior, a great lawyer, and a lot of faith."

"I thought you were going to say they finally proved you didn't do it."

"Ah no, that will never happen." She shook her head, lowering her eyes, trying to conceal the cloud of shame that shadowed them. "I confessed. My conscience is clear. I didn't *mean* to push him." Hesitating for a brief moment while she pressed her fingers over her closed eyes, and slowly rubbed them, like she was releasing the shame. She then let her hands drop back to the table and opened her eyes, revealing a light redness, that had appeared, but in a respectful tone, she did her best to continue, "I was trying to pull him down off the ledge, but he was so drunk, he almost took us both over. The window screen popped open, and to save myself, my reflexes made me push off the weight that was dragging me down."

Peter's lips parted so slight, as it finally started to make sense. He had never wanted to believe she could intentionally murder someone, but he could totally see Ambrose having an accident exactly how she had described. "I didn't know if your confession was true or where that came from."

"Yep, nothing too exciting to hear. Just a good old fashion accident caused by a stupid drunk being dumb, and I was unfortunate to be in the wrong place at the wrong time. That was my biggest mistake. The jury just didn't believe I was there innocently."

"That's what's been driving me crazy all these years." He motioned toward her with an inquiring hand. "How were you there? I didn't see you."

Exa bent her brows down when she looked back at him. "Sure, you did." Before she could continue, the barista came over and dropped off Peter's drink.

"Thank you," Peter said, while only offering the barista a side glance as they waited for her to leave them to their privacy.

Once she was gone, Exa leaned forward and said, "Remember when you came out looking for Doc to help you visit Ambrose?"

"Hmm, yeah, I guess." Peter felt his face pinch, wondering how Exa knew about that.

Exa continued, "He was talking to an old lady at the door."

"That was so long ago. I vaguely remember. Was there someone who used to live there or something?"

"No, that was me pretending to be someone else. I knew Ambrose would never let me inside the house, but I wanted to check on you for myself. It was just too easy. When Doc looked away, I slipped inside and hid."

Peter stared in astonishment. "What were you planning on doing?"

"I wanted to see you and try to get you to come home. Remember, I had talked to you on the phone, and I knew something was up."

"I don't believe it." Peter shook his head again, still so amazed how he had been fooled. "How did you end up fighting with Ambrose?"

"I followed you up the stairs and heard the whole argument. It made me furious. I was hiding in a room next to the bottom of the stairs. Pretty soon Doc came down, but Ambrose wasn't with him. Doc had left him to pass out. So after I saw Doc go back downstairs, I went up. I had to give Ambrose a piece of my mind. Everything else is a blur."

"I never understood how you had anything to do with it."

Exa smirked. "That makes two of us. I'm that unlucky."

Peter froze at the sight of her smile. It was sweet and soft, not a hint of the sarcasm he was used to. "You are so different. I can't get over it. You seem happier. If I didn't know better, I would say prison was good for you."

"I had a lot of time to fight my demons and bury some emotional stuff I'd been dealing with. When you are left in a cell with just your thoughts and memories, you have nothing left to do but face them."

"I just, yeah, you look great. I know I said that, but I can't get over the yellow dress. It's beautiful on you. I never expected it. It doesn't even look like you."

She smiled broader. "You know, I wore black every day for eighteen years."

"That's a long time to make a fashion statement."

"It was never meant to be a fashion statement. It was always my mood."

Peter raised an eyebrow. "Mysterious and forlorn?"

She thought for a moment and then said, "It was grief. I used to dress normal, until the day I said goodbye to you at the clinic."

Peter's chest tightened when he realized what she had brought up. She continued, "I always said part of me died that day. I went home and after lying in bed for days, I got up to get dressed, and the only thing that seemed appropriate was the black dress I had worn to my grandmother's funeral—I was in mourning."

Peter hung on to her every word as another mysterious layer that had always been Exa was peeled away. She continued, "After a few days of making the conscious decision to wear black, it became a part of me. When I went to prison and had to leave the black behind, I honestly had a nervous breakdown just changing my wardrobe. I did the whole shaky shoulders ugly cry and everything. I realized then I had been hiding my emotions in my OCD habits for so long, and as I fought off each habit, I healed a little."

"I had no idea the black was related to anything, let alone that." Peter let his eyes linger on hers, feeling a pull toward her from her recent admission. "I thought it was an artistic expression."

"No, it was an emotional expression—or suppression—I should say. And don't get me wrong, I'm not all the way healed, but I can put on a yellow dress and be okay with my past."

"Wow. All I can say is wow. I had no idea all that was going on."

"Most people have more to their stories than what they let on."

"I don't think most people have as much as you."

"Maybe not, but I'm glad you are in my story." She let her eyes drop while she continued, "I had a lot of guilt for a long time, and even after I learned you were alive, I had guilt over your health and so many other things. Now I know I must accept things as they are, and I'm grateful for my past now."

"It certainly is a unique one, isn't it?"

She looked back at him and said, "Phew, I'm still not good at talking about this stuff though," she joked as she wiped her forehead. "I think I'm sweating a little."

"I can't believe it's been six years. Where did the time go?"

"It went slowly for me. One painful mop bucket at a time."

Peter shook his head yet again, and said, "I can't get over how happy you look."

"When you've been given a second chance like I have, things take a different perspective."

"So now what are you going to do with all your free time in the real world. Another tour?"

She looked around the room like the answer to his question would be written on one of the walls. Then after a moment she said, "I honestly think I'm done with that life. It was a good run, but I can't handle the drama."

"Really?"

"Yeah, I'm getting older, and I realized how selfish my life has been. I want to make a difference in people's lives in a positive way. I realized something when I was in jail."

"What was that?"

"Do you know when I was the happiest in my life?"

"I would have guessed when you were performing, but the way you are talking I'm not sure. When?"

She held her eyes in communion with his and continued, "When I was watching you fall in love with playing the piano. I loved being your mentor."

"You were great at it." He pulled his lips into a half grin and teased, "Well, except for the moodiness."

"I deserve that. But, really, I was thinking about it, and I want to help you with your school. I think it would be good for me."

Surprised at the offer, Peter said, "I never did anything with the school. The house is still sitting there. Sometimes I take Lily over there and she roller-skates on the wood floor in the lobby. We race each other."

Exa laughed. "That's adorable. I can totally see that."

"I let her win, of course."

"Well of course you do."

Peter shrugged and then said, "I never got back around to completing the renovations or caring about it. I lost my inspiration for that after Gwen passed."

"Sorry about Gwen," Exa's voice lowered and then she added, "We all loved her."

Peter licked his lips and said, "I've made my peace with it." Then he pulled his lips into a genuine smile and said, "I get to see her every day through Lily."

"I bet you do. I know you're an amazing dad."

"I try. But, anyway, as far as the school goes, maybe that's what it needs — someone who is ready to take the lead on the project and get it going again. If you have a vision for it, I can get behind it."

"I do." Exa nodded, starting to show excitement about the idea again. "I totally understand now why you wanted to do it for the kids. I know the feeling you want to give them through music as the tool. I think together we can make it a reality, and I would love to be your project leader if you want me to."

"I always loved working with you. You know that. I think we make a great team."

"Great. Then it's settled. I'll head over there later today to see where everything is left off at."

"Perfect." Peter stole a look at his watch. "And on that note, I have someone I want you to meet, if you're up to it?"

"Lily," Exa said, her lips quivered slightly when she turned back to look at the door behind her. "Is she here?"

"Not yet, but she will be. My mom is bringing her. She took her out for pancakes, but they are going to stop back, and I can ask her to bring her inside, if you want to meet her."

"Of course, I do." Her eyes welled up with happy tears. "I can't wait to see her precious little face." Exa sat back into her chair, taking a sip of her coffee like everything in life was perfect as it should be. "That's exactly what I want to do today. Meet my granddaughter." Peter smiled back at her, knowing that Exa was finally going to be okay.

LATER THAT DAY, LILY PUSHED PETER'S WHEELCHAIR OVER THE PATH IN THE cemetery. Her blond spiraled pigtails bounced like springs as she chatted the whole way. "Daddy, how come I never met Grandma Exa before?"

"She got into some trouble and the police locked her up, but she was good, so she got to come home early."

"I like her."

"I thought you would. She was my favorite person when I was your age. She's the person who helped me to play piano."

"How come you don't play anymore?"

"I don't know. I just lost my reason to," he said sullenly. Then he smiled. "And also, because I spend all my extra time playing with my Lily Bean."

"Daddy, did you see that bunny over there!" she shrieked in excitement. "It ran over there!" She pointed to a group of evergreen trees.

"I didn't see it, but I believe you. If I were a bunny, I would like to live here too."

"Why?" She asked, her blue eyes brightened as they always did when she was so full of questions.

"Because it's full of trees and open spaces. It's a more natural habitat where not too many people come through to bother them." He grabbed the wheels on his chair, helping Lily push. She was feisty for a five-year-old girl and always insisted on pushing Peter, but it was difficult for her to push him for long distances and on uneven ground.

"Hey, you know what, Dad?"

"What?"

"When I grow up, I'm going to get a bunny."

"You want one for a pet?"

"Yeah, I think that would be cool. They're so soft."

"Well if you want, I can get you one now."

She stopped pushing, and jumped up, excited. "Can we call him Ruby?"

Peter could never say no to her, and every day she amazed him with the little things she did. "Whatever you want."

"Yeah! I'm getting a bunny! Oh, can I feed it carrots?" She frowned when he didn't respond, but his gaze was down and she didn't hesitate to follow it.

"Is this mama?" she asked. Although he came regularly to visit Gwen's grave, Lily had only come once two summers ago. She had been too young to understand it, and it was hard for him to try to explain things in simple terms to a preschooler. Lily knew who her mom was because they talked about her nonstop, but she understood Gwen to be in Heaven, so the graveyard thing confused her.

He nodded, and continued to look at the headstone he had memorized. Years ago, he had planted purple lilies and now they were grown in, stretching out, covering most of the ground. They were well over two feet tall and waiting to bloom.

"Here, put these on her stone." Peter handed a fresh bouquet of purple lilies to Lily. She took the flowers, gripping them in two hands, as the stems were thick. She weaved in next to one of the lily plants that was growing out of the ground.

"Dad, look!" She pointed to the headstone.

He inched forward, careful not to run over the lily plants. The lilies had multiplied like weeds and stuck out in every direction. It felt like wheeling through a small three-foot-tall jungle as he tried to see what she had pointed at. "Look what happened!" she said again.

In the center of the headstone was a heart with Gwen's name on it. It was modest and had been exactly what Gwen would have wanted, but it cracked down the center—probably from the winter moisture freezing inside. The crack started at the word "love" that was in her epitaph that read, "To know her is to love her." The crack split the heart, and out of the crack sprang a lily plant that had somehow weaseled its way to grow there. It was short and had one single blossom on it—the only blossom in the whole group of lilies as it was still early summer. The lily sat centered inside the broken heart.

"It's broken," Lily said in a disappointed voice.

Astonished, Peter let out a quiet breath, as he knew the opposite to be true. The lily had stretched to grow inside the broken heart—which had originally been made of hardened stone. Now the stone heart was adorned with the flower, making it more beautiful than it had originally been.

He sat in awe seeing the paradox that lay before him. His Lily— the little girl he never knew he wanted in his life—had done just the same. She snuck in, and she filled the hole in his hardened heart that was left by

Gwen. His heart would never be complete as it had been before, but somehow Lily made it even better.

She poked at the flower. "Should we pull it out?"

"Leave it." Now trying to hold back a tear, he said, "The heart's not broken anymore. The lily's mending it together."

Lily laid her flowers on the ground next to the budding lily. She giggled as she looked up. "Is that good?" Her blue eyes reflected the purple flowers and the joy she created.

"It's the best," Peter said. He suddenly had new inspiration that he hadn't felt in a while. Without dwelling in another moment of sadness, he knew what he needed to do and asked, "So, what do you say I show you the piano Grandma Exa gave me?"

Lily looked back at her dad, her brows were lifted in wonder. "You said you got rid of it?"

"It's in storage at her old house. I just thought of a new song to write. Will you help me?"

"Yeah, Daddy, let's go! I can't wait to see it. But let me say goodbye to Mommy." She bent down and put her face next to Gwen's headstone. "Bye, Mom. Love you. Don't worry. I'm taking care of Daddy." She kissed the stone next to the heart and jumped to her feet and ran behind Peter to push him back down the path. And asked, "Can I play the piano too?"

"Absolutely. I already know the name of the song we are going to write."

"Oh, what's that, Daddy?"

"It's going to be called, Lily in the Stone . . ."

The End.